Thad's evening was much more enjoyable with Dani sitting beside him.

There was just something about Dani Phillips he liked. She expressed her views in such a forthright way; it was refreshing. She was not happy about the possibility of tourists coming in and taking over her town, which came across loud and clear. But her opinion appeared at odds with what the city council seemed to want from him, and he could only hope that didn't cause a problem.

Dani had a job to do, and part of it was to show him around town. She'd already proven she could do it, even if she didn't agree with the council on their views on how to revive their town.

He had a job to do, and that was to decide if he could come up with a campaign to help draw tourists to this town. Potential problem? Not as long as he put a damper on his growing attraction to this feisty city manager. And dampen it he must. The last thing he needed was to fall for Dani Phillips.

JANET LEE BARTON and her husband, Dan, have recently moved to Oklahoma and feel blessed to have at least one daughter and her family living nearby. Janet loves being able to share her faith and love of the Lord through her writing. She's very happy that the kind of romances the Lord has called her to write can be read by and shared with women of all ages.

Books by Janet Lee Barton

HEARTSONG PRESENTS

HP434—Family Circle
HP532—A Promise Made
HP562—Family Ties
HP623—A Place to Call Home
HP644—Making Amends
HP689—Unforgettable
HP710—To Love Again

Don't miss out on any of our super romances. Write to us at the following address for information on our newest releases and club information.

Heartsong Presents Readers' Service
PO Box 721
Uhrichsville, OH 44683

Or visit www.heartsongpresents.com

With Open Arms

Janet Lee Barton

Heartsong Presents

Always to my Lord and Savior for showing me the way.

The Mississippi series was proposed before Katrina came along. It will take a longer book to tell her story. One day I hope to write the story of her aftermath in honor of all those who have dealt with the devastation. For now I dedicate this story to all of those who were in her path. I pray the Lord will be with you and that He continues to give you the strength, courage, and determination to rebuild your lives and your communities.

Our hearts and prayers remain with you always.

A note from the Author:
I love to hear from my readers! You may correspond with me by writing:

Janet Lee Barton
Author Relations
PO Box 721
Uhrichsville, OH 44683

ISBN 978-1-59789-375-6

WITH OPEN ARMS

Our mission is to publish and distribute inspirational products offering exceptional value and biblical encouragement to the masses.

PRINTED IN THE U.S.A.

one

Thad entered the offices of his advertising company, Cameron Concepts, feeling pretty good about the lunch meeting he'd just left. His instincts told him things had gone well, and if he was right he'd have a new account soon. Maybe Hanson had already left him a message.

But before he could even ask his secretary about it she handed him a memo. "You had a call from a Meagan Chambers while you were out. She asked me to tell you it is *very* important she talk to you as soon as possible."

Thad's heart seemed to stop beating for a moment as he took the piece of paper Linda handed him. He hadn't heard from Meagan in almost a year. . .not since he'd realized she didn't love him and he'd let her go as graciously as he could.

"Thank you, Linda." Thad went into his adjoining office, sat down at his desk, and studied the note in his hand. *Meagan. What could she possibly want?* Loosening his tie, he pulled it over his head and put it into the bottom desk drawer until he needed it again. *Only one way to find out.* He released a long breath and took note of the phone number on the paper once more before punching in the numbers. Swiveling his chair, he gazed out onto the Dallas skyline and waited for someone to pick up on the other end. He prayed nothing was wrong.

"Hello?"

Thad relaxed somewhat at the sound of Meagan's voice. She sounded fine. "Meagan? It's Thad. My secretary said you phoned me."

"Oh, Thad! Thank you for returning my call. I. . .Nick and I. . .want to ask a favor of you."

Thad wasn't sure he was willing to do any favors for his ex-almost-fiancée and her new husband, but he certainly was curious to find out what they wanted. "Oh? What is it you need?"

"Well, you know Magnolia Bay has been struggling for some time. That's one of the reasons I opened a shop here, remember?"

He did remember well. Meagan's small hometown was on the verge of dying because it had refused to allow casinos to open within its boundaries. As a result, some mom-and-pop businesses were forced to close their doors while the small tourist trade they'd once enjoyed had all but disappeared to the casino's luxury hotels and restaurants along the coast.

"Yes, I do."

"Well. . .ah. . .we've been making a little progress, but it is slow going and the city council has decided we need help."

"What kind of help?"

"Your kind. We need someone to help us sell our town. We need an advertising campaign."

Thad leaned back in his chair and closed his eyes. It was easy to remember Magnolia Bay as a charmingly quaint little town. "I see. And you would like me to put you in touch with someone in Mississippi who does—"

"No! We want you, Thad."

He didn't know what to say. It would mean going back and seeing Meagan again. Thad wasn't sure that was what he needed to do. The silence seemed to stretch along the phone line.

"Thad?" a masculine voice said. "It's Nick here. We really do need your help. Meagan has told everyone how you helped her business get its start and grow the way it has from the ad campaigns you created for her. We need someone we can trust to do this right."

Thad shook his head. He had nothing against Nick Chambers—other than he'd won the heart of the woman Thad had hoped to marry. But he'd been a decent guy, and Thad knew the man loved Meagan. He couldn't hate Nick. But Thad didn't necessarily want to work with him either.

"Thad, please just come to Magnolia Bay and talk to the city council before you say no," Meagan pleaded.

"That's all we ask, Cameron," Nick added.

They were both on extensions, double-teaming him. "Hey, you two don't play fair." Thad chuckled.

"Oh, it's worse than you think, my friend. We're triple-teaming you," another familiar voice said.

"Cole? Is that you?" Cole Bannister had been a good friend and brother in Christ. They'd attended the same church in Dallas until Cole had fallen in love and moved back to Magnolia Bay. Suddenly this seemed *way* too much of a coincidence. . .that Meagan and Cole had both moved to the same town in Mississippi. . .and they were both asking for his help now—

"It's me. We need you, Thad. You know we wouldn't ask if we didn't," Cole said. "We've made some headway.

Several new businesses have opened up, and we've been able to draw in a few more tourists—but it's not nearly enough. We need someone who knows what to do, what angle to use. I have a room at Bay Inn with your name on it. Please say you'll come and talk it over."

Thad couldn't turn them down. He and Cole and Meagan had been good friends, and he'd missed them. But, even more important, they were brothers and sister in Christ. He had to go.

"Let me look at my calendar." Thad glanced at his desk. He had some free time coming up. "I can be there in a week. Will that work?"

"Yes!" the triple chorus assured him.

❧

"I know you don't like this idea very much, dear," Claudia Melrose said from across Dani's desk, "but the town council voted to hire Thad Cameron to help us find a way to keep this town alive, and we need your help in convincing him to take on the job."

Dani Phillips, Magnolia Bay's city manager, sighed and pushed her reading glasses up on her nose. She knew Claudia was right, but she still wasn't happy about having to show the Texas man around town. "It just bothers me that we had to go out of state to find someone to help us when I'm sure there are advertising companies right here in Mississippi that would know our needs better."

"And would they even want to bother with a tiny town on the verge of extinction?" Claudia shook her head. "I don't think so. Most of them are too busy trying to make a living of advertising the casinos in the area—the very thing that threatens our existence. Besides, Thad Cameron is well qualified and comes with great references. He helped Meagan turn her Color Cottage into a thriving business. She knows him well. And Cole says he's a great guy. They all went to the same church in Dallas, you know. I think that's the Lord telling us this is the right thing to do."

Dani couldn't suppress a loud sigh. "Well, I hope you are right. We can barely pay for city services now. I hope this isn't a big waste of our money."

"Dear, just trust that the Lord knows what we need. Either Mr. Cameron will take the job, or he won't. We'll know before too long. He's arriving tonight, and I'd like you to come to dinner and meet him. Cole and Ronni will be there, of course, and Meagan and Nick."

Dani didn't want to go. She didn't want to meet Thad Cameron, and she certainly didn't want to show him around town the next few days. But she was the city manager, and the city council had voted. She really had no choice. Besides, Claudia had become a second mother to her, and the woman had been through so much, losing a son and then finding out he'd gambled nearly all of the family money away. She'd even had to turn her home into a bed and breakfast just to be able to keep it. No way would Dani refuse her invitation. "What time do I need to be there?"

"About six thirty will be fine." Claudia glanced at her watch. "I'd better be going. He'll arrive any time now, and I want to be home to welcome him."

"Is he staying at the inn?" Dani asked.

"Yes, he is. I've heard wonderful things about him, and I'm sure we're going to like him, Dani."

"I just hope he's right for Magnolia Bay."

Claudia slung her purse over her arm and headed toward the door. "I'm sure he will be. I feel like this is an answer to our prayers. I really do. Bye, dear. I'll see you tonight."

"I'll be there."

"Good," Claudia said as she left the office.

The thought of having to show the Texas man around had Dani's head throbbing. The slight headache she'd awakened with quickly grew into a full-blown one. She'd heard all the rumors. He'd almost been engaged to Meagan Evans, now Chambers, until she'd come home to open her business and fallen in love with her high-school sweetheart all over again. She and Nick seemed very happy, and Dani just hoped this man wasn't coming back to cause problems. From all accounts he was very successful in Dallas and probably had all the business he needed right there in Texas. Why would he be coming to help out a town he knew nothing about. . . except to see once again the woman he'd wanted to marry?

Her head pounding with hammer force now, Dani rummaged around in her desk drawer until she found a bottle of aspirin. She downed two tablets with the cold cup of coffee on her desk and leaned back in her chair. Taking off her reading glasses, she rubbed the bridge of her nose and sighed. She truly dreaded the next few weeks. But she'd get through them with the Lord's help. Sliding her glasses back on, she tried to concentrate on the reports on her desk, but to no avail. Dani did the only thing she knew would help. She prayed.

Dear Lord, please help me accept that I have to show this Thad person around. Please let him have Magnolia Bay's best interest at heart and not be coming here to make trouble for Meagan and Nick. We do need help. We barely have enough money to pay our city workers, Lord. I love this town, and I know You do, too. We did the right thing by turning down the casinos that wanted to locate here—I know we did. But our town has paid a deep price. You know what we need, Lord. Please help us. In Jesus' name, amen.

Dani felt better. Everything would be all right. The Lord was in control. She pulled the reports toward her and got back to work.

ə

Thad had been driving for hours when he crossed the Louisiana-Mississippi state line. He could have flown, but he wanted the freedom of having his own car. Besides, he hadn't taken off any time since he'd last visited Magnolia Bay. He wasn't sure who was crazier—Meagan and Nick Chambers for asking him to come back, or him for agreeing to go. He couldn't explain it, but with their asking and Cole's providing a place to stay he somehow felt he was meant to help them out. His last visit had been painful, though, and he hoped this one would find his heart healed and Meagan happy. Thad thought he was over her, but until he saw her with her new husband he couldn't be sure. He prayed he was and that he could be truly happy for her.

Leaving the interstate, he drove down to Highway 90 so he could travel along the coast, his thoughts on Magnolia Bay. While his visit there had been short, the town had lingered in his memory. It was almost picturesque and had a hometown feel. . .the kind of place anyone would like to be from. He remembered wishing he could stay longer, get to know the people there. Well, now was his chance. *If* he was truly over Meagan and felt he could help, he'd see what he could do. He'd created a lot of successful advertising campaigns, but trying to sell a town would be a whole other realm. Still, he did love a challenge.

It was a sunny day, and the sunlight gleamed on the water to his right as he glimpsed beautiful older homes amidst magnolia trees and moss-draped oaks on the left. One town seemed to run into another until he saw the sign to Magnolia Bay. It was on a small inlet just off the Gulf of Mexico, and the water seemed a little bluer as he made the turn onto Bay Drive, the main street in town. He passed by Meagan's Color Cottage and was pleased his heart didn't jump or his pulse speed up. He knew he'd see Meagan and Nick at the inn that evening, and that would tell him for sure if he was over her. Again he prayed he was. Otherwise he didn't think he could help the town. It would be much too awkward to work with Meagan and her husband.

He followed the directions Cole had given him to get to Bay Inn and was impressed as he drove around a curve to see the large inn overlooking the bay below. Cole had told him that his wife Ronni's former in-laws—Cole's aunt and uncle—owned it. And, when Ronni's husband, Brian, died, she had moved in with Claudia Melrose.

They'd found out Ronni's husband had gambled nearly everything away, leaving them both in a bind, and Cole had been called in to help his aunt decide what to do. To keep her home, Cole had suggested she turn it into a bed and breakfast. From the looks of it Thad thought they'd made the right decision.

He pulled in the drive and was barely out of the car before Cole came out to meet him.

"Thad, it's great to see you! I can't thank you enough for agreeing to come help us out."

As they shook hands, Thad felt the need to clarify things. "Now, Cole, I've made no promises. I've only agreed to talk and think about it."

Cole grinned and slapped him on the shoulder. "I know—I know. But once you realize how badly we need your help I'm certain you'll agree."

"Oh, you are, are you?" Thad laughed and shook his head. "We'll see."

He grabbed his luggage, and Cole led him into the inn.

When Thad walked inside he felt as if he'd stepped back in time. A wide foyer ran from the front to the back of the house, with double doorways opening to rooms on each side. Detailed molding framed the floor and high ceiling which boasted a mural he wanted to study at length. He could only imagine how lovely the rest of the inn was.

"Oh, this is beautiful, Cole. How long did you say it has been in your aunt's family?"

"It was built around 1850 as a summer home to get away from New Orleans. And the Melrose family had used it as that up until around 1940 when they decided to make Magnolia Bay their year-round home. Everything is original to the home except the kitchen and the bathrooms, our third-floor living quarters, and the new elevator. We had to do some remodeling when Aunt Claudia decided to turn it into a bed and breakfast."

Thad nodded. "It's certainly been well maintained."

"Yes, it has. The Melrose family loved this home. But it is very large for this day and time. Aunt Claudia seems happy she can keep it and make a good living at the same time."

An auburn-haired woman came through one of the doors near the end of the long foyer, and from Cole's expression as he watched her approach them Thad knew who she was even before Cole introduced her.

"This is Ronni, my wife," Cole said. "Ronni, this is Thad Cameron, one of my very best friends."

"I'm sorry I wasn't able to come to your wedding, Ronni," Thad said as he took her extended hand and shook it. He'd sent a gift but felt it was too soon after his breakup with Meagan to come back for Cole's wedding and see her again. Instead he'd made excuses he was sure fooled no one.

"We understood." Ronni smiled at him. "But I'm so glad to finally meet you—Cole has told me so much about you that I feel I know you already. He's missed you."

"Well, Dallas hasn't been quite the same since he moved away. I've lost my golfing partner, but I was playing too much golf anyway." Thad smiled at Ronni. "I can certainly see what drew him out of Dallas for good. And he looks content. I'm happy for the two of you."

"Thank you," Ronni said as her husband put his arm around her.

"I knew you'd understand once you met Ronni. She's a keeper," Cole said, drawing his wife a little nearer.

The front door opened just then, and a lovely older lady rushed inside. "Oh, dear. I knew that must be your car, Mr. Cameron. I am so sorry for my tardiness. I meant to be here to welcome you."

"Aunt Claudia, you aren't that late. He only just arrived." Cole smiled at the woman and led her over to Thad. "This is Claudia Melrose, Thad. She's the owner of Bay Inn and the matriarch of this family." He chuckled when his aunt gave him a playful punch then added, "She's also a member of the city council."

"How do you do, Mrs. Melrose?"

The small woman had an elegant air about her, but when she spoke Thad could tell she was down to earth.

"Oh, please call me Claudia." She waved her hand. "We don't use last names much in this part of the country."

Thad smiled at the older woman. Soft silver curls framed her face, and her blue eyes were bright and lively. He nodded. "I'd be honored. But only if you'll call me Thad."

"Agreed." She nodded. "I hope you'll be comfortable here at Bay Inn, Thad. We started out providing only breakfasts, but because so many of our guests have requested it we've recently started serving dinner, too. Sometimes we join them, and sometimes we eat in our private quarters. Our guests are on their own for lunch, and some prefer to dine out for dinner, too. But you're different. You're a friend of the family, and we'd like you to take your meals with us. We'll be having dinner around six thirty or seven. I can't thank you enough for coming to Magnolia Bay to see if you can help us."

"Thank you for providing me with a place to stay and for making me feel so welcome. . .Claudia." Thad still didn't feel right about calling this lovely older woman by her first name.

"I'll leave Cole and Ronni to show you around. If you

need anything just let one of us know. I'm going to check on our dinner now. We have a new cook, and sometimes she needs assistance."

She swept down the hall and disappeared through a doorway.

"If you don't mind I'm going to see if I can help Claudia. She and our new cook don't always see eye-to-eye," Ronni said with a grin. "I'll leave you and Cole to catch up, and he will show you the room we've picked for you, Thad. I hope you'll like it."

"I'm sure I will. Thank you for your hospitality, Ronni."

She shook her head. "We're more than glad to have you here. Thank you for coming. Magnolia Bay needs your help. I'll see you at dinner."

She gave her husband a quick kiss before following Claudia to the kitchen.

"Come on. I'll show you to your room." Cole picked up one of Thad's cases and led the way upstairs. "You know, *you* may think you only agreed to come here to talk, but as far as my wife and aunt are concerned you're already hired."

Thad had a feeling his friend might be right.

two

By the time she got home from work Dani's headache had finally eased up enough that she thought she might make it through the evening. She was still dreading having to spend the next few days with a stranger, but she had to admit she was curious about this Thad person. And she loved going to Bay Inn. The old home was meant to be filled with people, and now that Claudia had turned it into an inn it always was. She decided she might as well try to make the best of things as she went to get ready for the evening.

After a quick shower she applied a minimum of makeup and dried her curly black hair, coaxing it around her face with her fingers. Short as it was, it took only a few minutes, but she was glad she'd decided to cut it a few weeks ago. It would make the summer heat easier to handle—if that was possible. Summer in south Mississippi seemed unending some years.

Dani dressed in one of her favorite outfits, one she wore to church often. It was an amethyst and white jacket dress that brought out her violet eyes—or so she'd been told. At any rate meeting new people always made her nervous. She felt that she needed all the confidence she could muster for the meeting tonight, and looking her best certainly wouldn't hurt.

When Dani left home she'd almost convinced herself she was looking forward to the evening. She always enjoyed being with Cole and Ronni and Nick and Meagan, but thoughts of Nick and Meagan had her thinking of Thad Cameron again. By the time she arrived at Bay Inn, she found herself praying once more that his visit didn't lead to trouble for the couple.

❧

Thad strolled over the grounds of Bay Inn after getting settled in his room—the view off his balcony was so tranquil and beautiful that it pulled him outside. He'd found it peaceful to walk along the trail overlooking the bay. The incoming breeze that came up the bay cooled the afternoon heat, and as Thad took a deep breath of the air he wondered once more if he'd lost his senses by coming back here. He couldn't help but be a little apprehensive about meeting up with Meagan and Nick again. Just how did one act around the woman who'd chosen an old love over him? The one and only time he'd been in this town was when he'd had his heart broken. He prayed that once he saw Meagan again he would know his heart was truly healed.

Now, as he headed downstairs to meet up with Claudia Melrose and the Bannisters, Thad was impressed to see guests mingling there and in the sitting room across from the guest dining room before dinner. Cole had told him they would be eating upstairs in the family quarters, but his aunt liked to be on hand before dinner to visit with the guests and make them feel at home.

"There you are," Cole said when he spotted him entering the foyer. "We're just waiting for Nick and Meagan and

Dani Phillips to arrive. Then we'll go upstairs to the family dining room."

"Looks like you must be filled to capacity," Thad said, looking around at the small clusters of guests.

"We've been that way since the grand opening."

"Well, that's a good sign for the town."

Cole nodded. "It is. It's shown us people are out there wanting something quieter than the casino attractions when they come to the coast. But while we can market the inn, and Ronni has done an excellent job of that, we don't know how to market the town as a whole. That's why we need you, Thad."

Thad was relieved to be saved from replying when his hostess waved to someone over his shoulder.

"Dani, you are right on time," Claudia called out to the young woman who stood just inside the foyer. Claudia rushed over to her and pulled her across the room to stand in front of him. "Dani Phillips, meet Thad Cameron. Thad, this is our city manager, and she'll be showing you around town the next few days."

She was petite and slender, and her short dark hair curled around her small oval face. But it was the color of her eyes that Thad knew he would never forget. They were a light purple, and he'd never seen that shade of eye color before. He wondered if she might be wearing contacts. In any case, she was quite—adorable was the word that came to his mind, but he wasn't sure it fit. He only knew something about her had his attention from the moment her gaze met his.

"It's good to meet you, Dani," Thad said, holding out his

hand to shake hers. He was surprised when the touch of her hand in his sent a shock of electricity up his arm and straight into his chest. He thought maybe she'd felt it, too, when she quickly slid her hand from his grasp.

"It's nice to meet you, Mr. Cameron. I hope I'll be able to answer all your questions about Magnolia Bay."

"I'm sure you will. I look forward to your showing me around, and please—call me Thad." The fact that she would be the one to help him explore the town made the idea of working in Magnolia Bay appeal to him. He'd have to ask Cole whose idea it was to have her be his tour guide. . .and be sure to thank them.

"Oh, I don't know—"

"I'm *so* sorry we are late." A familiar voice pulled his attention away from Dani Phillips for the moment. "We dropped Nick's sister, Tori, and a friend off at the movies."

Thad would know that voice anywhere. He turned to see Meagan and Nick Chambers heading their way. She looked much the same as when he'd last seen her, only better. A light shining from her eyes all but shouted how happy she was, and Thad was more than a little relieved that he could truly be glad for her. It meant he was over her.

"Meagan. . .Nick. It's good to see you," he said honestly as Nick held out his hand for him to shake.

"I'm glad to hear you say that, Thad. We're thankful you've come back to help us all out," Nick said.

Meagan stood there for a moment as if she were trying to tell if they were still friends. Something in his expression must have given her the answer she needed because her smile broke into a grin. "It is so good to see you, Thad. We need your help, my friend, and there is no one better than you to find a way to market a whole town."

"Whoa now. I haven't agreed to do this yet."

"I know. But you will," Meagan assured him with a smile.

Thad had a feeling she was right. And maybe he could, now that he realized he was over her. Oh, he still cared, but it was as the friends they'd started out to be and not as someone still in love with her.

"She can be pretty persuasive when she wants to be." Nick turned to Thad and grinned before adding, "But you already know that, don't you?"

Thad laughed at Nick's frankness, and he was glad he could call the other man a friend, too. "Yes, I certainly do."

"I guess it's time we took this meeting upstairs," Cole said. "The guests have already found their way to the dining room, and it's our turn to eat."

They all took the elevator up to the family quarters on the third floor, where they found a large buffet waiting for them.

"Looks like Ada has outdone herself," Ronni said.

"Ada?" Meagan asked. "You have a new cook?"

"We do. Marge became a grandmother and moved to Jackson to be closer to her daughter and that new baby. Ada has only been with us a few weeks, but she's very good."

"She is. But she's also bossy. Doesn't like anyone in the kitchen with her," Claudia said.

"She and Mom don't exactly agree on how to prepare things," Ronni said, grinning at the older woman.

"We agree on practically nothing," Claudia said. "She doesn't like it when I suggest a different way of doing things. I only try to make things easier for her, but she thinks I'm trying to interfere with the way she runs the kitchen."

"Now, Aunt Claudia, you *do* like to keep tabs on that kitchen." Cole chuckled.

"Well, of course I do. It used to be *my* kitchen, after all," Claudia said, lifting her eyebrow. "But she is a very good chef," she conceded with a smile.

Thad was relieved when everyone at the table laughed. For a minute he thought there was going to be an argument. From the expression on Dani's face she was as relieved as he was.

"Don't mind me," Claudia said. "I've just been having a problem giving up cooking for the guests. Ada is a great cook, and if I learn to stay out of her way we'll get along fine. But that's enough about me and our new chef. We have much more important things to talk about."

She motioned to the buffet set out on the sideboard. "Please, everyone, fill your plates and find a place at the table. Once we're seated, I'll ask Cole to say a blessing. Then we can get this dinner meeting underway."

Thad helped himself to the glazed ham and sweet potatoes, adding a biscuit to the side of his plate before he took a chair next to Dani.

Cole took his seat and said the blessing for the meal. "Dear Lord, we thank You for this day and our many blessings. We thank You for bringing Thad here safely, and we ask that You show him how badly we need his help.

We thank You for this food we are about to eat, and we especially thank You for Your Son and our Savior. In Jesus' name we pray, amen."

There wasn't much conversation for the first few minutes of the meal. Obviously Ada was an excellent chef, but Thad wasn't sure whether to comment about it or keep his thought to himself. He was glad when Ronni spoke the words for him.

"Mom, while she's not quite as good a cook as you are, this is all really delicious. Since you have way too much to do with making our guests feel welcome and with your work on the city council, I think we need to do all we can to keep Ada happy."

"You have a point there, dear. I'll work on it." Claudia grinned and changed the subject. "Now who wants to be the one to explain why we need Thad to help us out here, or do you want me to?"

"I don't think anyone can explain it better than you, Aunt Claudia," Cole said.

"All right then." Claudia looked over at Thad and smiled. "Thad, being from Texas, I'm sure you know tourist business is very important along the Gulf Coast."

Thad had only to nod before she continued.

"Well, the townspeople of Magnolia Bay figure this part of the coast has more than its share of casinos. We decided to refuse to let any of them locate in our city limits a long time ago—and we've paid a price for it. With their huge buffets and luxurious accommodations, exciting shows and gambling, what tourist trade we once enjoyed seemed to pull away. Many of our small mom-and-pop companies were forced to close due to lack of business, and it looked as if our town would shrivel up."

"And it just about did," Cole said.

Claudia nodded. "Many of the people along the coast have suffered because of the casinos. I lost my own son to their lure." She shook her head and sighed before her gaze met Thad's once more.

"But the people in this town have decided to fight for it and for what we believe in. We're trying to bring new businesses in and draw those tourists who would like a more peaceful Southern setting than what casino life offers. We know they're out there. We need your help in letting people know we welcome them and that Magnolia Bay is here—to offer tourists a different choice."

When she stopped and smiled at him Thad wasn't sure what to say. He'd always liked a challenge, but this could be a huge job.

"Well, Thad? What do you think?" Cole asked.

Thad shook his head slightly. "I don't know. I'm not sure I'm the man for the job—I've never tried to sell a whole town before."

"Oh, you're up to it, buddy," Cole said. "I know you, and you love a challenge."

"I do. Still. . .I don't think—"

"Just let Dani show you around. Get to know our town before you say no," Meagan insisted.

Thad's gaze took in everyone at the table. They all looked so hopeful and appeared confident he could do the job—well, all but Dani. She didn't meet his gaze, and he wasn't sure what she thought. All he knew was that he had to look into it. They'd asked for his help, and he couldn't turn them down without at least seeing if he could provide what they needed.

He looked over at Dani. "What time do we get started, Dani?"

"We can start first thing in the morning. Meet me at the coffee shop, and we'll go from there."

"Only if you let me buy you breakfast." Thad's heartbeat seemed to stop as she hesitated before giving him an answer.

After what felt like minutes but was probably only seconds, Dani nodded at him. "I like their omelets. But I do have an early meeting. Will nine o'clock be all right with you?"

"It's a date then. And nine will be fine," Thad said, his heartbeat thudding again and steadily increasing speed at her acceptance. That alone was enough to have him rethinking about working in Magnolia Bay. He'd never had quite so strong a reaction to anyone in his life. . .not even to Meagan. They'd just started out as friends. Dani was a total stranger to him, and that made his attraction to her even more disconcerting.

That and the fact he had no intention at all of letting himself fall for another Magnolia Bay beauty. All he had to do was look across the table and see Meagan and Nick to be reminded of the heartache that could come from letting himself care about another Mississippi woman.

❧

Dani tried to will her heartbeat to slow down as Thad Cameron smiled at her. She hadn't been prepared for her first reaction to him. The current of electricity that had bolted through her at his handshake had left her pulse racing. And it still hadn't slowed down.

Thad was very nice looking, tall, with dark brown hair and eyes the color of chocolate. But something more than his looks had her struggling to keep from staring at him. Maybe it was because she was trying to discern if he was here to help her town or because of Meagan. He seemed perfectly at ease around her and Nick, but still—he'd almost been engaged to the woman not that long ago. Could he be so accepting of her happiness with another man? Somehow Dani didn't think so. Maybe he just hid his feelings well.

At any rate she was aggravated she was spending so much time thinking about the man sitting beside her when she didn't want to show him around and didn't want him selling her town as a new tourist spot. She didn't want the tranquility of Magnolia Bay to change.

But she'd been hired as the city manager and had a job to do. She only hoped she could get her racing pulse settled down before the next morning.

three

Thad was awake early the next morning. He'd gone for a late-night run along the trail on the inn's property and slept soundly. But he was anxious to tour Magnolia Bay and try to find the right kind of hook for an advertising campaign. He had to admit he was looking forward to seeing Dani Phillips again. He had to see if her eyes were as purple as he remembered.

Cole had given him directions to the coffee shop the night before, and as Thad came downstairs and stopped in the foyer he hoped the breakfast he'd be treating Dani to would be as good as the one the guests at Bay Inn were enjoying—if aroma had anything to do with it.

Claudia spotted him on her way into the dining room. "Thad, I don't know why I didn't insist on Dani meeting you here for breakfast. It would have been much easier on you."

"Not a problem, Mrs. Melrose. It will probably be easier for Dani to meet me in town. That way we can start our tour right after we eat."

"Oh, please, you must call me Claudia, or if you can't bring yourself to do that, then adopt our custom of putting miss before my name."

"As in 'Miss Claudia'?"

The older woman's face broke into a smile. "Oh, yes, just like that. It sounds much better, don't you think?"

"Yes. As a matter of fact I do." He did like it. It sounded less formal and yet respectful at the same time. "Thank you, Miss Claudia."

"You are welcome. I'll see you later in the day and find out what you think of our town."

"All right, see you then. You have a good one."

"You, too. Say hello to Dani for me."

"I will," Thad assured her as he headed out the door. The sun was bright overhead, and a light breeze was coming off the bay. But it was late June, and he had a feeling it was going to be a warm, humid day.

Thad got to the coffee shop before Dani and found a table by a window so he could be on the lookout for her. He ordered coffee while he waited for her to arrive. The café was full of people who all seemed to know each other, and he couldn't help but think how nice it must be to live in a town where you knew most of the inhabitants from when you were young. . .and where you would all grow old together.

It was a little ironic to him that two of his best friends from Dallas now lived in this small town. There must be something to this place. Cole and Meagan both seemed quite happy in Magnolia Bay. Of course they'd found true love here.

And he'd left it here. No. That wasn't true. If what he thought he and Meagan had together was true love, she wouldn't have chosen Nick over him. Thad had wanted it to be the real thing, but it couldn't have been. He sighed and looked out the window. He wasn't sure he knew what true love was or if he would ever take a chance of finding out again. While he was happy for Meagan, he couldn't forget how much it had hurt to be rejected by her. He didn't want to experience that kind of pain again.

Thad was so into his thoughts that he never noticed when Dani entered the coffee shop. Only when she slid into the booth across from him did he realize she'd arrived.

"I'm sorry I'm late," she said. "The emergency preparedness meeting I had to attend ran long."

"Emergency preparedness?"

"Yes." She smiled at him. "This time of year it would more aptly be called hurricane preparedness."

"Already?"

She looked at him and shook her head. "If you were from Galveston instead of Dallas, you'd probably understand. Hurricane season starts in June and lasts clear through November."

"Whew. That's a long time."

"It's a very long time."

"I guess I knew that, but over in Dallas we worry more about spring storms producing tornadoes."

"We worry about those, too, just not nearly as much as the ones spawned by hurricanes." She gave the menu a glance before the waitress came to take their order.

"What do you recommend?" Thad asked as the waitress pulled out her pen.

"I'm having the country omelet. It's full of ham and onions and peppers. And I'd like some hash browns on the side and a cup of coffee, please."

Evidently she didn't have to watch what she ate to stay so small. "Mmm, sounds good." He looked up at the waitress.

"I'll have the same thing."

When she left to put in their orders, Thad glanced over at Dani and noticed she was wearing glasses. She slid them off her nose and into a case in her purse. That answered his question—or at least he thought it did. She didn't wear contacts—not unless she wore the colored ones that didn't need a prescription. But somehow he didn't think so.

He tried not to stare, but her eyes were beautiful—even more so with the light of day.

"No," Dani said as if he'd asked a question.

"No what?" he asked, but Thad had a feeling she knew what he was thinking.

"I don't wear contacts."

Thad had to laugh. Obviously he hadn't been successful in his effort not to stare. "You've been asked that more than a time or two, I suppose?"

She grinned at him. "You suppose right. But I never have, nor do I ever intend to wear contacts." She shook her head. "I can't even put drops in my eyes. I'd never be able to get one in."

"I don't think I could either. But you *do* have lovely eyes."

"Thank you." Dani's gaze met his for a moment before she broke eye contact and looked out the window.

"You are welcome." Thad had a feeling his compliment had made her feel a little uncomfortable and decided he'd better get the conversation on a less personal topic. "What are you going to show me first?"

"Well, you've found one of the best-kept secrets already. This coffee shop used to be an ice-cream parlor, but it's become a gathering place for the locals now. And the food is great. Not quite as good as that at Bay Inn, but I like it. As for what next, we can walk around the downtown area so you can see what other places of business we have. And I can show you some of the residential sections, too. It would be great if we could draw more people to make their home here."

"That will probably happen if you can draw the tourists."

She sighed and nodded. "That's what the city council thinks."

"And what do you think?" He sensed she didn't agree with the council

Dani shrugged. "We need something to help our tax base grow. So I'll do my job and show you the town and—"

"I have a feeling showing me around is something you'd rather not do," Thad said. He thought he might be right as he saw her cheeks flush a soft pink.

"I—I would rather not have tourists overrunning our town, and I'm not sure that's the way we should go. But I could be wrong. At any rate I've heard that if anyone can come up with a way to bring more people to our town, it's you." She smiled over the cup of coffee she held to her lips.

"Well, I've never tried to market a whole town before. I'm not sure I'm the man for the job, but I said I'd see what I could do so—"

The waitress brought their breakfast then, but Dani went ahead and finished his sentence for him.

"So we'll both keep our word and tour the town as soon as we eat."

"So we will," Thad said with a smile before he popped a bite of omelet into his mouth.

≈

By lunchtime Dani knew it was going to take longer than she had figured to show Thad Cameron around town. It seemed more than half the town had heard about the plan to hire an advertising firm to help revive Magnolia Bay, and they all had an opinion on how Thad should go about it.

She had to admire him, though. He let each and every person they ran into tell him what they thought he should do, listening carefully and even taking notes as if their opinion would be considered when he started to work on an ad campaign.

"You won't really take this free advice you're receiving, will you?" she asked as they crossed the street and began to walk down the boardwalk along the bay.

He shrugged and grinned. "You never know. You'd be surprised what you can come up with, taking bits and pieces from all that advice." He motioned to the water lapping along the shore. "It is quite beautiful and peaceful here."

Dani nodded. "That's what I love most about it. From here you'd never know that just a few miles up the Gulf Coast there's a different feel. Sadly, many people like that lifestyle better than what Magnolia Bay has to offer."

"I'm getting hungry. Mmm. . .and I smell burgers. Where is it coming from?"

"From Beach Burgers. . .just around the bend."

"Want to grab some lunch?"

"Might as well. We have to eat sometime. But I'll pay for mine this time."

"No, ma'am, you won't. You are doing me a favor. I'll pay for your meals when you are with me."

"Thad, it's not really a favor," Dani admitted. "It's part of my job."

He smiled at her. "Even more reason I should pay for your lunch. I'm sure you have other things you could be doing."

Dani had a feeling she was fighting a losing battle as they neared the hamburger stand. The aroma only improved, the closer they got.

They both gave their order, with Thad pulling out his wallet before she could even unzip her purse.

"Thank you," Dani said as they went to sit at one of the outdoor tables to wait until their burgers and fries were brought to them.

"No, thank *you*. I know you must have a lot to do, and I appreciate your taking the time to show me around—job or no job."

His smile had her pulse racing again, and she was getting more than a little frustrated that she had no control over slowing it down.

"This is nice," Thad said as a light breeze floated in from the bay. "I can't remember the last time I ate lunch outside."

"Neither can I." Dani rarely took a lunch hour. She didn't have time. She usually ate at her desk, going over paperwork or getting ready for a meeting.

"What exactly is it a city manager does? I would imagine it's a big job."

"It's one I've always wanted. And, yes, there is a lot to do. I guess the main thing is that I'm responsible for the entire administration of the city government. I have to prepare and recommend an annual budget to the city council, administer and secure the enforcement of all the laws and ordinances of the city—or, in other words, make sure the police department is manned and doing its job—and I negotiate contracts for the city." She smiled at him as their lunch was brought to the table.

"Whoa! That's some job you have!" Thad sounded impressed.

Dani chuckled. "That's just to name *some* of my duties. There are reports and recommendations to the council at their request and—"

"Not to mention showing total strangers around town when you probably have a pile of paperwork to do. I'm sorry to add to your work load, Dani."

He sounded so sincere that Dani felt bad for resenting the time she was giving to him. She shrugged. "It won't go anywhere. It will wait until I can get to it. Besides, this is part of my job too." She took a bite of her burger and looked out over the bay.

"Well, I'll tell you what—I don't want you to get too far behind. Would it be easier for us to do this kind of part time, so you can work in your office part of the day?"

None of this was his fault, and he'd been very considerate of her. Dani rushed to reassure him. "Don't worry, Thad. I'll get my other work done. Actually this is a nice change of pace for me. I might have to start taking a real lunch hour from now on. I think I could get used to eating outdoors."

❧

Thad was certain he could get used to eating outdoors too, if it meant sharing a meal with Dani. But he had a feeling her idea of having lunch outdoors didn't include him. She was being gracious, but he had a feeling the last person she wanted to share a meal with was him.

Maybe that would change over the course of the next few days. And yet, he told himself, he had no business hoping it would. He didn't need to become more attracted to her. But he admired her. She was trying to help her city—even if the way the city council had decided to do things was not how she would like them to be done. He respected her for that—and for her honesty about it.

"Where do you think we should go next?" he asked as they were finishing up their lunch.

"We can tour a little more of the downtown area if you'd like. Maybe tomorrow you can see some of the outskirts and the residential section—explore the beach a little more. Whatever you think will help you best." She wadded up her hamburger wrapper and took a last sip of her drink before throwing it all in the trash receptacle.

"Okay. Let's explore downtown a little more this afternoon." Thad threw his trash away too, and they headed back toward town along Bay Drive.

Dani pointed ahead. "We have a new florist that just opened, and it's next to Meagan's Color Cottage. Do you want to stop by her shop?"

"Let's check out the flower shop. I can drop by Meagan's anytime. Besides, I know what her shop is about." He grinned at her. "I'm glad it's become such a success over the last few years."

"I hear you are mostly responsible for its taking off so quickly."

"Well, I don't think I'd go that far. But I am glad the advertising campaign worked so well."

The Waters Flower Shop was nice. It was in a quaint cottage a little smaller than the one that housed Meagan's shop. With its window awnings and a white picket fence outside, it seemed the right place for a flower shop. The owners were a middle-age couple, Brad and Lydia Waters, who were setting out on a new adventure, and their enthusiasm was obvious as they showed him and Dani around.

"What made you decide to start your own business?" Thad asked as they showed him the greenhouses out back where they grew much of their stock.

"Our youngest child got married, and Brad retired."

Brad chuckled. "We didn't quite know what to do with ourselves. Then the city council started trying to draw businesses into the city, and, well, we wanted to do our share to help. We love Magnolia Bay. We don't want to see it die out."

"How is business?"

"Better than we expected. The locals are very supportive, even though there are several other flower shops in town."

"What makes you stay here?"

"It's home," Lydia said. "We wouldn't want to live anywhere else."

As the afternoon went on, one thing became evident. Wherever they went, everyone they talked to had one thing in common—love and loyalty for Magnolia Bay.

four

When Thad left Dani at her office, they'd made plans to meet for breakfast the next morning. . .with a little persuasion from Thad.

"We both have to eat."

"But Claudia will have a great spread at Bay Inn you can enjoy, and I can eat at home."

"We'll get an earlier start if we meet for breakfast."

Dani shook her head and opened her mouth, but Thad interrupted before she could say no. "Please, Dani. I feel bad enough about taking you away from your work. Let me treat you to breakfast. It's the least I can do."

He was rewarded with a chuckle and a nod. "All right. We'll meet for breakfast."

"See you then," Thad said. "Please don't work too late."

"How do you know I'm not going home?" Dani asked.

"Just a feeling I have. Are you?" He quirked his eyebrow at her.

"No, not yet," Dani admitted. "I need to check on a few things first."

"That's what I thought."

She grinned and shrugged.

"As I said—don't work too late, okay?" Thad had a feeling she was going to do exactly that, though.

"Okay. Enjoy your evening."

Dani probably agreed quickly so he would leave. But Thad was having a hard time doing that, and he didn't know why. "See you tomorrow."

"See you then." She took the matter of leaving out of his hands as she turned and walked into city hall.

Thad headed toward his car. He might as well drive back to Bay Inn—Miss Claudia was probably waiting for a report of his day.

He was right. When he arrived at the inn she was talking to the receptionist in the foyer. As soon as she spotted him she took him to the office she shared with Ronni, who was nowhere to be seen at the moment. "Would you like some coffee or tea, Thad?"

"No, thank you, Miss Claudia. I'm fine."

"I've been anxious to see what you think of our town! Please have a seat and tell me about your day."

Thad took a seat in one of the chairs flanking the fireplace, and Miss Claudia sat across from him. "I think Magnolia Bay is one of the most charming towns I've ever seen."

Miss Claudia clapped her hands together. "I'm so glad. I was sure you would like it. Dani showed you what you wanted to see?"

"She did—at least as much as we could get in today. I asked a lot of questions of the people we ran into, and that took awhile. But we'll start out again tomorrow. She's an excellent tour guide."

Miss Claudia nodded her head. "I knew she would do a good job. She's a wonderful city manager."

"I feel a little bad about taking her away from her work, but she told me showing me around is part of her job." He didn't tell Miss Claudia that statement had stung just a bit. He'd have preferred it be something she wanted to do and not something she looked at as work, but beggars couldn't be choosers.

"She's not sure how she feels about our plan, but she's a loyal employee of the city council and will do the best she can to let you get a feel for Magnolia Bay. And Cole and Ronni have plans to give you a taste of one of our nicest restaurants this evening."

"Are you coming with us?"

"Not this time. I'm playing hostess here."

"We'll miss you," Thad said. He really had taken a liking to the older woman. She reminded him of his mother in some way he hadn't figured out yet.

"I'd like to join you. But when I turned my home into a place of business I promised myself I would be here most evenings with my guests. And I do love it. Having people in this house all the time has added joy to my life."

"I understand."

"You'll be in good hands with Ronni and Cole. And you'll love it. Anything on the menu is quite good."

"I've had some great food in this town already. I think I'm going to have to make use of your walking trail out back while I'm here."

"That's what it's for, dear," Miss Claudia said. "You have a good time this evening, and I'll talk to you later."

By the time Thad had changed clothes and joined Cole for a jog along the shady trail then showered and changed again, he'd worked up an appetite and was looking forward to the evening.

He met Cole and Ronni downstairs, and they took him to the Seaside Surf and Turf to meet the owners and their good friends Mike and Alice Benson. They were some of the first locals, along with Meagan, to heed the call from the city council to help revive the town.

It appeared they'd made the right decision for the town and themselves. Their business seemed to be thriving, if business on a weeknight was anything to go by. Once their meals reached the table, Thad could understand why. His butterfly shrimp were large and succulent, fried to perfection. The almond rice pilaf served with them was excellent too.

"Is your clientele mostly local, or have you been able to draw in tourists from the casinos down the coast?" he asked Mike.

"Our locals are loyal; but word has managed to get out, and lately we seem to be seeing more tourist trade. Some have even asked about accommodations in town and how we've stayed a secret so long."

"A secret?"

"It seems many people don't have a clue we're here anymore. Of course, being set off on the bay instead of right on the gulf, we're a little out of the way, but not that much if they know where we are," Mike said. "Most of the people who've found us are staying in Biloxi or Gulfport but have no interest in gambling. They're mainly there to see the old houses on Highway 90 and enjoy the history of the area and not the lively night life."

"Why do you think Magnolia Bay has been bypassed?"

"Most tourist guides are selling the casinos and what they have to offer. And when our businesses started shutting down there wasn't much of a draw. We didn't know how deeply having casinos in our area would affect us until it was almost too late to do anything about it. Thanks to Miss Claudia and Mike's mother and Meagan's grandmother, the council finally decided something had to be done to save this town," Alice added.

"Well, it looks like this town has a definite will to fight, from what I've seen today," Thad said.

"How did your tour with Dani go?" Ronni asked. "We should have asked her along tonight."

Thad wished he'd thought of that. He'd enjoyed her company today and was looking forward to the next day. "It went real well. We toured a lot of the downtown area, but there's more to see. I'd also like to drive along the coast and see what the competition is like so I can draw some strong comparisons."

"Oh, you'll find plenty," Alice said. "The old homes along the coast are lovely, but sadly big business has taken over a lot of the areas where some of them were wiped out with past hurricanes."

Ronni nodded. "Now there are just more restaurants and motels to go along with the casinos and their luxury accommodations."

"Something for everyone—except for those of us who long for things the way they used to be, for the slower pace, the tranquil atmosphere," Cole said. "I can remember when most of the restaurants and businesses along the coast were like Mike and Alice's place—home-owned and home-operated—and unique and memorable."

"It's not that way anymore. Only a few of them have been

able to hang in there and make it against the others."

"Do you think you're going to be able to help us, Thad?" Cole asked.

"I don't know yet. I hope so." And he did. He felt drawn to something about this town and its people.

❧

Dani stood and stretched. She'd done all she was going to do today. It was nearly eight o'clock in the evening, and she was more than ready to call it a day. But she'd managed to finish several purchase orders and start a report on her time spent with Thad Cameron, in case the council members asked for one. In her short time as city manager she'd found that most of them, especially Morris Gentry and Ed Jenson, liked reports of just about any kind.

Too tired to think about cooking, she placed an order for shrimp scampi at the Seaside Surf and Turf before heading out to her car. As she drove out of the parking lot and turned onto Bay Drive, she wondered what Thad was doing this evening. More than likely he was enjoying a delicious meal at Bay Inn with Claudia and the Bannisters.

Sharing meals with him today had been more enjoyable than she had imagined. And, much as she hated to admit it, she was looking forward to showing Thad around the next day. She told herself she had no business enjoying spending time with him—he was only here to do a job. And she no longer wondered if he was here because of Meagan.

Last night at Bay Inn, even though she didn't know what he felt about Meagan and Nick, he'd seemed genuinely happy to see them together. And today, when she'd asked him if he wanted to visit Meagan's Color Cottage, he didn't seem uncomfortable at all, and his response made perfect sense. After all, he did know the shop well.

She was relieved it wasn't a problem. He'd been so easy to be around today, and she liked the way he took time to hear what each person had to say, listening as if their opinions mattered to him. And maybe they did. She hoped so. She loved this town and the people in it, and she hoped Thad would see how special Magnolia Bay was.

Dani found a parking place at the Seaside Surf and Turf, grabbed her purse from the car seat, and went inside the restaurant to pick up her order. She'd handed her money to the cashier when she heard her name from across the room. Looking over in the direction of the voice, she wasn't prepared to see Thad hurrying toward her.

"I knew you were going to work late. You're just now going home, aren't you? I knew I should have—"

"I just did a little catch-up, that's all."

"And now you're going home to eat all alone."

"Well, I do that a lot, Thad. I live alone."

"Yeah, well, so do I. But it's not all that much fun to eat alone, is it?" He didn't wait for an answer to his question. "Why don't you come join Cole and Ronni and the others? We've just begun our meal."

She shook her head. "No, I don't want to intrude. . . ." But she looked across the room to see everyone at the table motioning for her to join them.

"Please join us. Besides, I feel like a fifth wheel tonight. You'd be helping me out."

Dani hesitated a minute. Really, all that was waiting for her at home was an empty house and television to keep her company while she ate. She knew everyone at the table, and she was relieved Nick and Meagan weren't part of the party. "All right, I'll join you."

"I'll have your order sent right over, Miss Phillips," the cashier said, the carryout box she'd been about to hand Dani still in her hand.

"Yes, please do that. And thank you," Dani said, looking back as Thad waited for her. Mike had pulled up a chair from another table, and they'd all made room for her to sit at the large round table.

"Good to see you, Dani!" Alice said as Dani took the empty seat Thad held for her between him and Alice.

"It is. We were just all saying you should be here."

"And I was kicking myself for not asking you," Thad said as he sat back down in his seat. "Now that I know you worked so late, I really do feel bad. I just figured you'd seen enough of me for one day."

"I told you I was only doing some catch up. I work late a lot of days." It did seem to bother him that she'd worked overtime, and she didn't want him to blame himself. "My job isn't your normal nine-to-five, and I like it that way." *It fills up the hours since Dad passed away.* But she didn't say that. Instead she said, "It's the job I've always wanted."

"Which is exactly why the city council was so excited about hiring you," Cole said. "They knew you would give this job your all—at least Aunt Claudia was sure of it."

"And I was glad to have her in my corner. She and my parents were good friends."

"Yes, she's mentioned them often," Ronni said.

Dani's meal was set before her, and they all went back to

enjoying the excellent dishes the Seaside Surf and Turf was becoming known for.

"You know—if you draw more tourists into town, you may have to enlarge this place," Cole said to Mike.

"I've thought of that. But what I'm hoping is that as we draw tourists more people will move into town and someone else will decide to open another kind of restaurant. And then we'll have enough business to go around."

"That's how it works a lot of the time," Thad said.

Dani sighed. "I just wish we could bypass all those tourists."

"You aren't happy about that aspect of growth, are you, Dani?" Ronni asked.

"Not really. But I can see where a lot of people in town think that's the answer for us."

"But you don't?" Alice asked.

"I like the feel of Magnolia Bay as it is. Knowing people and having them know you. I'm afraid we're in danger of losing some of our Southern charm, just as some of the other towns along the coast have." As silence descended on the table, she felt as if she might have said too much. Dani took a bite of her scampi and told herself not to be so vocal.

"I hadn't thought about things that way. That is something to consider," Ronni said.

Everyone looked thoughtful, and Dani hoped she'd given them *and* Thad more to think about too. It was one thing to bring more people here to live, and she wouldn't mind tourists who enjoyed the kind of town Magnolia Bay was. But she prayed the essence of her hometown would stay the same.

Thad's evening was much more enjoyable with Dani sitting beside him. There was just something about Dani Phillips he liked. She expressed her views in such a forthright way; it was refreshing. She was not happy about the possibility of tourists coming in and taking over her town, which came across loud and clear. But her opinion appeared at odds with what the city council seemed to want from him, and he could only hope that didn't cause a problem.

Dani had a job to do, and part of it was to show him around town. She'd already proven she could do it, even if she didn't agree with the council on their views on how to revive their town.

He had a job to do, and that was to decide if he could come up with a campaign to help draw tourists to this town. Potential problem? Not as long as he put a damper on his growing attraction to this feisty city manager. And dampen it he must. The last thing he needed was to fall for Dani Phillips.

five

The next week seemed to speed by as Dani showed Thad around Magnolia Bay and the surrounding area. They had visited every shop and business in the small town by Thursday. Then they set out down the coast line on Highway 90 so Thad could get an idea of what drew the tourists along the rest of the Mississippi Gulf Coast.

Dani offered to drive so Thad could act as a sightseer himself. She proved to be a great travel guide, pointing out sights she thought he might want to get a picture of and stopping so he could.

The grand old homes caught his attention from the start, and he wondered what it would have been like to live in one when it was first built as a summer home to get away from New Orleans.

But he also noticed the hotels, motels, and fast-food restaurants taking up a lot of land in between the short stretches of lovely homes.

"Camille was a category five hurricane. She came right across this area and left only steps in some cases. Some of these homes are pretty, but they're built new to look old. The truly old ones are the ones with character and have survived many storms."

"And a five is how strong?" Thad asked.

"It has winds in excess of 155 miles an hour."

"Whoa."

Dani nodded. "A category one has winds from 74 to 95 miles an hour, a two is from 96 to 110, a three is from 111 to 130 miles per hour, and a four is from 131 to 155. After that it's all a five."

"What would happen now that so much has been built up here and along the coast if another huge storm comes?"

Dani shuddered. "It would be catastrophic. I don't want to think about it. It's a constant fear in all of us, especially at this season of the year. It could happen anytime. We just pray our warning systems will help prevent loss of life. I'm afraid we can't avoid losing property, though, even with stricter building codes."

Thad could tell she was shaken by his question. "How long does the season last again?"

"From the first of June until the end of November. . . this year, next year. . .every year." Dani sighed. "It's a long season. They've predicted this one will be very busy."

"They? The National Weather Service?"

She nodded. "The hurricane center in Florida and other specialists—just about everyone who studies hurricanes for a living—all seem to be saying the same thing."

"What does that mean for you as city manager of Magnolia Bay?"

She gave a short laugh. "Tension. . .and lots of it. . .for months. Worry that if a big one comes we might not be ready. Fear that I might not be able to keep calm when I'm needed most. Worry that some of the old-timers won't evacuate or get to safe shelters. We've had lots of storms since Camille, and Magnolia Bay has had its share of damage, but none of them has been as devastating to the coast as Camille."

"I take it the fear is that another one as bad as Camille will hit this part of the coast again?"

She nodded. "Or one even worse. . .and that people living here have become complacent and won't leave in time."

Thad could see how a huge hurricane would cause more destruction on the Mississippi Coast now than even Camille had back then. The huge casinos and their hotels were right on the water. Restaurants and other businesses were just across the highway. The area wasn't built up as much when Camille hit. Thad shook his head and sent up a silent prayer that there wouldn't be one worse.

"I'm sure you'll do fine," he tried to assure Dani. "But I hope nothing that bad comes your way."

"It's only a matter of time. Anyone who resides on the coast lives with that knowledge. Once a hurricane gets into the gulf, it will hit somewhere. And poor Florida has had its share of storms in the past few years. Pensacola is still recovering from several of them."

Thad felt a prickle at the back of his neck just thinking about it. Hurricanes were something he'd given an occasional thought to, but only after Meagan and Cole moved to the area. He would never again take lightly news of one in the gulf.

By the time they reached Pascagoula, Thad was glad to turn his car around and head back to Magnolia Bay. It wasn't that these towns along the Gulf Coast weren't pretty, for the older neighborhoods were—those where old homes still sat regal amongst moss-draped oak trees and massive magnolias. And a lot of the businesses were located in serene settings, nestled beside those same kinds of trees that once stood guard over homes no longer there. The restaurants, shops, condos, and hotels with views of the gulf would draw many, he was sure. But it was the almost untouched charm of Magnolia Bay he wanted to return to.

He could certainly see why Dani wouldn't want her hometown to give in to the tourist trade in the same way. Obviously some people were happy with the growth and business the casinos had brought into their area, but he was sure others were saddened to see their hometowns change so drastically through the years.

Suddenly Thad decided that if he took on the advertising campaign for Magnolia Bay he would do all he could to help maintain its charm. It was something he needed to give a lot of thought to before bringing any ideas to the city council.

For the moment, though, he wanted to enjoy the rest of the day with Dani, who was beginning to occupy far too many of his thoughts. He looked forward to meeting her each morning for breakfast and spending the major part of the day with her, and he dreaded the time when she'd tell him she could no longer be his tour guide because she'd shown him all there was to see of Magnolia Bay. He had a feeling it was going to be soon.

On Sunday he attended church with Miss Claudia, Cole and Ronni, and Meagan and Nick. He was pleased to find Dani attended the same church.

Miss Claudia tried to talk her into coming back to Bay

Inn for Sunday dinner, but she begged off saying she had a lot to do

Thad didn't doubt she was telling the truth. He'd been taking up a lot of her time lately. But he found himself wishing she had accepted the invitation.

❧

By the time Thad met with the city council at the beginning of the next week, Dani knew her stint as tour guide was coming to a close. She told herself she would be much better off if he refused the job offer and went back to Texas. But as she spent more time with him, seeing his interest in her hometown grow, she didn't think that was going to happen.

She sat in on the meeting on Monday and listened as Thad told the council he would agree to develop an advertising campaign for Magnolia Bay.

"Oh, Thad, I'm so glad you've decided to do this for us," Claudia said.

"We really do appreciate it," Morris Gentry added.

"I may not be able to come up with an idea you like, but I'll do my best."

"We've heard all about you, through Claudia and Cole and Meagan," Ed Jenson said. "We have every confidence you'll be able to help us."

Dani had no doubts he could come up with a great advertising campaign. She'd been paying more attention to the one he'd created for Meagan's Color Cottage and could see why her business had taken off so quickly. The commercials were classy. Her fear was that Thad's ad campaign would be *too* good.

"Thank you all," Thad said. "I have several ideas but need more time to develop them. I need to return to Dallas after the Fourth of July, but I'll get on it as soon as I can. This may take a little while, though. I've never tried to sell a whole town before, and it will require just the right hook. But once I work up several ideas I'll be back to present them to you."

"You take all the time you need, Thad," Claudia said. "We want this done right."

"Yes, we do," Morris said, with several other council members echoing him.

"Well, I want to do it right too. I do thank you for asking your city manager, Miss Phillips, to show me around. She proved to be a wonderful tour guide, and I feel I know Magnolia Bay much better for her efforts."

Dani could feel her cheeks warming at his compliment. She hadn't expected it but was grateful for it. She still felt as if she had to prove herself to some of the councilmen and women.

As the meeting came to an end, Dani felt a little disappointed. Much as she thought she would be relieved not to have to show Thad around town anymore, she was finding she had mixed emotions about it.

She'd been trying to deny she'd looked forward to meeting Thad for breakfast the last few days. But each morning when she spotted him waiting in a booth at the coffee shop and he looked up and smiled that special smile of his, her pulse had told her the truth.

Now she knew she would miss seeing him every day. And yet, while he was gone, she would find some relief in not having to hide her growing attraction to him. For she was attracted to Thad—in spite of the fact that if he took the job the city council offered him he would be trying to do the very thing she didn't want—bring more strangers to Magnolia Bay.

"Dani," Claudia called to her after the other council members had shaken Thad's hand and left the room. "I wanted to invite you to join us at Bay Inn for the Fourth of July. We're treating our guests and some friends to a cookout and watching fireworks go off over the bay. You will join us, won't you?"

"I. . .yes. . .I'd like that, Miss Claudia. Thank you."

"Good. We'll eat around seven, and fireworks are scheduled to start at nine."

"I'll see you then," Dani said. "I guess I'd better get back to my office. I have some work to catch up on."

"Dani," Thad said as she headed out the door.

"Yes?"

"I'm glad I'll get to see you again before I leave. And I meant what I told the council. You've been a wonderful tour guide. Thank you."

"You're welcome. It was a nice change of pace," she admitted.

"Added to everything else you do I'm sure it was a change. I'm not sure how nice it was, though. But I do thank you. You made discovering Magnolia Bay an adventure."

Dani didn't know what to say next, so she just nodded her head to acknowledge his compliment and waved before hurrying down the hall to her office. Oh, yes. She was going to miss showing Thad Cameron around town.

❧

Thad watched Dani blush at his compliment. He hadn't run across many women who still did that in this day and time, and it was refreshing to see. Made him want to say something else to see that color deepen, but Dani was out the door before he had a chance. He suddenly felt alone. He would miss meeting her for breakfast, miss sharing lunch at Beach Burgers with her, and just plain miss spending most of his days with her.

It was probably a good thing he had to go back to Dallas—could be he needed to put some space between himself and the town's city manager.

He turned to see Miss Claudia watching him, but if she had an inkling of what he was thinking she didn't let on.

"Are you ready to head back to the inn, Thad? I think Ada was making brisket for dinner tonight."

"Yum. That sounds wonderful to me. Let's go."

"I'm glad you'll have a couple of days before you return to Dallas and that you're celebrating the Fourth of July with us. You haven't had much of a chance to relax."

Thad thought back to the past week—spending time with Dani and discovering Magnolia Bay. The week had been different for him, a definite change from being in the office, from his daily routine—but Miss Claudia was right. It hadn't been exactly relaxing. Enjoyable, exciting, yes. But the word that came to mind concerning his time spent with Dani was. . .distracting. At times in the past week those lovely eyes of hers had distracted him from the reason he was in Magnolia Bay.

Something about her had him wondering what she was

like as a child or if she wanted children or if—

"Thad?" Miss Claudia brought him out of his thoughts. "You ready to go?"

"Oh, I'm sorry, Miss Claudia. Yes, I'm ready. And I was about to say it's been a very enjoyable week for me. I almost hate for it to end."

"Well, I'm glad to hear that," Miss Claudia said as they left the building and headed for their cars. "And you don't have to come back only for business purposes, you know. You are welcome here anytime. We have an extra room in the family quarters, and you'd be more than welcome to stay there."

"Why, thank you, Miss Claudia. That means a lot to me."

"I can tell you've come to appreciate Magnolia Bay, and I know you'll come up with an advertising campaign that is just right for our town. *That* means a lot to me and to us all."

As Thad followed her back to Bay Inn, the responsibility he'd taken on felt heavy on his shoulders until he realized that, as always, the Lord would give him the right idea at the right time. All he had to do was ask. He sent up a silent prayer doing just that.

Dear Lord, please help me to find the right hook, the right idea, to help this little town. The people here stood strong against the big casinos, but they've paid a price. Please help me find the best way for them to revive this town as You would have it done. In Jesus' name I pray, amen.

Dani prepared to go to Bay Inn for the Fourth of July festivities with one ear tuned to the weather forecast. A tropical storm had formed in the Atlantic, and while most weather models on television projected it heading out to sea, one or two showed it going into the gulf.

She closed her eyes and sent up a prayer that it would stay in the Atlantic and pose no threat to any land mass. She did so dread the next few months. Living on the coast this time of year could be wonderful, but at the same time nearly everyone had that quiver of apprehension in the back of their minds during hurricane season.

The warnings were wonderful—she couldn't even imagine what it must have been like back in the days when they had no warnings at all. But in this day and age of knowing a tropical system was forming, though still able to predict only so far into the future, the early warnings carried with them their own set of problems. There were days, and sometimes even weeks, of watching and waiting, depending on how slow the system moved and what the prevailing weather patterns were.

Dani flipped off the television and grabbed her purse. It was early yet. No need to worry too much now, she told herself as she headed out the door to her car.

Although the day had dawned hot, humid, and heavy, it was turning out to be a beautiful Fourth of July. A light rain had fallen about noon and cooled things down a bit, leaving a breeze behind to keep it that way.

She looked forward to the cookout and seeing the fireworks display. . .and to being with friends. She tried to tell herself it had nothing to do with seeing Thad again, but deep down she knew better. She'd missed him yesterday—more than she thought she would.

She pulled up at Bay Inn just behind Nick and Meagan

and joined them as they made their way to the back of the house. Inn guests and friends of the Melrose and Bannister families gathered in the lovely backyard where the smell of grilling meat intermingled with the scent of the waxy blossoms of the magnolia trees. Flowers bloomed everywhere, and tables with umbrellas had been set up all over the grounds. Ronni came to greet them.

"I'm so glad you could all make it," she said. "But where are Tori and your grandmother, Nick?"

"They'll be here anytime," Nick said, looking back in the direction they'd come. "I hope."

"If we seem a little nervous, it's because Tori got her license yesterday and is driving. Gram offered to ride with her—she has more patience with her than Nick does." Meagan chuckled. "Or me either."

"We tend to make Tori too nervous," Nick admitted. "Where are Cole and Thad?"

"They're down by the bay, setting out fireworks for tonight," Ronni said. "I'm sure they'd be glad for you to join them."

"Go on, honey," Meagan said. "Tori will be here any—"

"There they are now," Ronni said as Tori and her grandmother rounded the corner of the house.

The relief on Nick's face was plain for all to see. "Okay. I'll go see what Cole and Thad are up to." He gave his sister and grandmother a wave as they stopped to talk to Claudia and bent to give Meagan a quick kiss before going to find the guys. "See you later."

"He's like a mother hen sometimes, the way he looks after us all," Meagan said. She shook her head and smiled.

"But I wouldn't have it any other way. I love the man he's become."

"That's kind of obvious," Ronni said. "I think it's great that you and Thad have remained friends, though. He and Nick seem to get along great too."

"It would be very hard for anyone not to like Thad," Meagan said.

That it would, thought Dani. She'd even come to like him. . .a bit too much for her own comfort. She needed to put him out of her mind.

He was going back to Dallas soon, and after that, while he'd be coming back and forth over the next few months, he would eventually return to Dallas for good. It was time she reined in her growing feelings for the man. His home was in Texas, and hers was here in Mississippi. They had no future together.

But it wasn't long before she realized that was easier said than done. When Thad came to stand beside her to watch the fireworks display later that evening, her pulse sped up and her heart began to beat erratically. No, it certainly wasn't going to be easy to rein in those galloping feelings—especially when he touched her shoulder and she turned to find him looking at her intently. For a moment she thought he might kiss her.

six

Thad enjoyed the Fourth of July. Not only was it good to be with friends again, he was glad Dani was included in the group. He'd missed her the day before. He'd almost gone to her office to ask her to have lunch with him, but he'd occupied so much of her time in the past week and a half that he was sure she had to catch up on some work. Still, he'd gone to Beach Burgers on the off chance she might show up for lunch. She didn't, and it wasn't the same without her.

Now, as they stood side by side, watching the fireworks shoot off over the bay and rain down above them, Thad wished he had the right to put his arm around Dani and perhaps tilt her face to kiss her. . .as Cole had just done with Ronni. It wasn't the first time he'd thought of doing that, but Dani had never given him a hint she might want him to. And it was probably best that way. Much as he felt he belonged here, his home and business were in Dallas and her life was here.

Besides, he'd been hurt once and was thankful he'd gotten over Meagan and could be happy for her now. But he wasn't ready to test the waters again. Still, there was something about the small woman at his side that had him wishing he was.

Maybe if. . . Thad put his hand on Dani's shoulder, and

she turned to him with a smile. His heart thudded in his chest.

"You're leaving in the morning, Thad?" Nick asked, bringing him out of his thoughts and back to the reality of the here and now.

"Yes. I have to get back to Dallas and finish up several projects. I'll be back in a few weeks, though." He glanced at Dani, but she'd turned away, which was probably for the best. More than likely he'd have gotten his face slapped if he'd done what he wanted to do and kissed her. He breathed a sigh of relief that he'd escaped that humiliation, and yet. . .were her lips as soft as they looked?

"You're welcome here anytime," Cole said. "It's felt sort of like old times having you here with Meagan and me."

Thad nodded. "I should be angry. You both up and moved away and left me to fend for myself." He grinned to let them know he was teasing—well, half teasing.

"If you stayed in Magnolia Bay long enough, I think we'd get you to move here too," Cole added. "Something about this town draws people to it once they've been in it awhile. Our problem is letting them know we're here."

Thad nodded. He had to agree the town had a pull to it. The problem was, he didn't know if it was Magnolia Bay or the town's city manager that had him dreading to leave the next day. All he knew was it wouldn't be easy to return to Texas.

❧

Thad looked out at the Dallas skyline, trying to come up with a hook for the Magnolia Bay ad campaign. But it was hard to zero in on what he wanted to do. It hadn't taken him long to know for sure he was definitely over Meagan. He wouldn't be spending so much time thinking about Dani if he weren't. Even now he couldn't seem to get into the swing of things for thinking about Magnolia Bay and the young woman who'd been taking up a major space in his thoughts.

"Mr. Cameron?" Linda peeked around the office door, bringing him out of his musings.

"Yes, Linda?" She had a worried look on her face, and Thad motioned for her to come in. He pointed to the chair in front of his desk. "Sit down. Is there something I can do for you?"

"I'm fine. But—are you all right? You haven't seemed quite the same since you came back from Mississippi."

"No?" He hadn't thought it was that obvious, but it certainly was the truth. He didn't even feel like the same person, and he was afraid he never would be.

"You've seemed a bit distracted, and I wanted to make sure you're all right."

Thad couldn't deny being distracted lately, but he wasn't ready to tell her about Dani. "I just have a lot on my mind. I've been asked to work up an advertising campaign for a small town in Mississippi, and it's not coming easy."

"Oh. Will you be going back there soon?"

Good thing she didn't ask if he *had* to go back. "I might. It depends on if I can get a handle on how to develop the campaign."

"What kind of town is it?"

"It's really charming. As if it's been untouched over the years. The people live at a slower pace and are very nice.

It's hard to explain, but it's kind of like the hometown everyone would like to call their own."

"It sounds nice. But if it's that appealing, why does it need to advertise?"

"Well, it's surrounded by other towns that said okay to letting casinos in their city limits, and they've all prospered to the detriment of Magnolia Bay. For a while it looked as if the town would die out."

"Oh, how sad, especially since they were trying to do the right thing."

Thad nodded. "The city council has been trying to turn things around for the past few years, and it looks as if they're succeeding to a degree. Some of the people who had moved away have come back to help. And now they want me to come up with something to draw tourists to their town."

"Well, I'm glad things are all right with you," Linda said, getting up from the chair. "I can see where this would take a lot of thought, but if anyone can do it you can."

"Thank you, Linda." For the first time Thad noticed she seemed a little jittery, as if she wanted to say something more to him. "Tell me, what's been going on with you while I've been out of town? You still seeing Lance?"

Linda blushed and smiled. "Well, yes, I am. And, ah, Lance and I got engaged on the Fourth of July." She held out her hand for him to see a large diamond on her ring finger.

"Wow! That's some ring, Linda. Congratulations. Lance is a lucky man."

"Thank you. We're planning a winter wedding."

"You aren't thinking about quitting, are you?"

"Not yet." She grinned at him. "At least not until after the wedding."

"I see. You're preparing me for that eventuality?"

"Sort of. . .we're talking about it. Lance doesn't much want me to work after we're married."

Thad nodded. "I see. Well, I won't worry about finding a new secretary yet, but thanks for letting me know I'll have to one of these days."

"I'm sorry—"

Thad laughed and shook his head. "No, you aren't."

"Well. . .not totally. But I will miss working for you. You're the best boss I've ever had."

Thad shook his head as she closed the door behind her. First Meagan left for Mississippi and found an old love, and now his secretary would be leaving the firm for her love. Would he ever find a woman who felt that kind of love for him?

He sighed and ran his hand across his forehead. Just one more thing for him to think about. But he had enough on his mind at the moment. He'd deal with replacing Linda when the time came. Meanwhile he had several projects to focus on before he could dive into the Magnolia Bay proposal. And right now he needed to clear his mind and get to work.

❧

The next week seemed to drag by for Dani. She hadn't realized how much she'd enjoyed spending her days with Thad. Now that he'd gone back to Dallas and she had no chance of running into him, she missed him more than she'd expected to.

It was wonderful showing him the Magnolia Bay she loved and seeing it through his eyes while he was here. He'd liked it a lot, she felt sure of that. And if he hadn't been hired to "sell" her town, she thought maybe he'd feel as she did about drawing tourists to it. But he'd accepted the job, and now she could only pray he'd find a way to help it keep its charm.

She stopped by the grocery store to pick up something for supper and was trying to decide whether to grill a small steak or a chicken breast when she heard her name. She turned to find Meagan rolling her buggy toward her.

"Dani! It's good to see you. Nick and I were just talking about you last night."

"Oh?"

"Don't worry—it was all good," Meagan said, smiling. "He was saying you're doing a great job as city manager and he was glad the city council chose you."

"Why, that is nice to hear. Please thank him for me."

"I will. I guess you've been busy catching up this week, after showing Thad around all last week. Did you get behind much?"

"It wasn't too bad," Dani answered.

"I'm sure Thad will come up with what Magnolia Bay needs. He's very good at what he does."

"I've seen your ads for your Color Cottage. They are great."

"Thad gets the credit for building my business through those ads. They're excellent." Meagan smiled openly at her. "You knew I was nearly engaged to Thad when I came here to open my second shop, didn't you?"

"I'd heard—"

"Oh, yes, I'm sure I was the talk of the town for a while. But when Nick walked back into my life I knew that what I felt for Thad wasn't the kind of love it needed to be if I was thinking of Nick all the time. But Thad seemed to know that even before I did. He nudged Nick to let me know how he felt about me. We're grateful to him for bringing us to our senses and getting us back together."

Dani didn't know what to say and was relieved she didn't have to say anything as Meagan continued.

"I felt horrible for hurting him, but I'm thankful we've managed to remain friends. He's special to both Nick and me."

Dani was still at a loss for words, but Meagan didn't seem to notice.

"We're thinking of having a cookout when Thad comes back into town. We'd like you to come too," Meagan said. "We thought it would be fun to get everyone together again."

"Thank you," Dani said. "I'd love to come. Just let me know when." She would be glad to know when Thad was coming back to Magnolia Bay.

"I will. You haven't heard when he'll be back, have you?"

Obviously she wasn't going to find out from Meagan. She shook her head. "No, Claudia hasn't mentioned it."

"Hmm, maybe Nick and I will call him and see when he thinks he'll be here. I'll be sure to let you know when we set a date for the cookout."

"Thank you, Meagan. I hope no storms will be out there to mess up things."

"We're all praying about that. I hate this time of year," Meagan said. "I'll talk to you later."

"Okay. See you later." Dani waved good-bye. It seemed that most of the residents of the Gulf Coast could be heard echoing Meagan's sentiments at various times throughout hurricane season.

❧

Later that evening, as Dani grilled her steak, she thought how nice it was that Meagan wanted to include her with their friends. She'd been a couple of years behind them all in school, but even if she'd been in the same class she wouldn't have been active in their circle. She couldn't have been.

Her mom passed away when she was in high school. So between going to school and rushing home to keep up with the wash, clean the house, and cook dinner for her dad, she didn't have time to hang out with friends. In fact, she had no time to socialize.

But she didn't mind. She'd been shy during her school years and deep down still was. She had to make an effort to be more outgoing, especially as Magnolia Bay's city manager. And it wasn't too hard, at least not during working hours. She told herself it was part of the job she loved so much, and besides, she'd known most of the people in town all her life.

Only when she stepped into a social atmosphere did she have problems. It wasn't that she'd never been asked out; it was more that she wasn't confident enough in her dating skills to try them out. Most of the time she gave a lame excuse for not being able to go, and the few times she'd accepted and gone out on a date she'd regretted it.

She found she felt older than most of the men she went out with or that they were expecting more than she was willing to give. Finally it had become easier not to date than to worry about it. But since spending so much time with Thad the last week, she'd started wondering what it would be like to go on a date with him. Somehow she didn't think it would be like the others. She thought she might enjoy it. But that was unlikely to happen, and she didn't need to waste time thinking about it. Seeing him at Meagan and Nick's was entirely different from being asked out on a date with him.

It *was* nice to think about spending time with Meagan and Nick and Ronni and Cole and their other friends, though. She did get very lonely since her dad had passed away, but she didn't dwell on it too much. It would be nice to be included with friends she respected so much. And. . . she couldn't deny she would look forward to seeing Thad when he came into town. No, she couldn't deny that at all. But he wouldn't be coming here to see her, and she needed to remember that.

Dani let out a deep breath. She did miss him, though. She missed meeting him at the coffee shop, missed taking an afternoon break at the snow cone stand as they'd done a couple of times. She hadn't even been able to go back to Beach Burgers knowing it wouldn't be the same. Now she found herself looking forward to his return and wondering how she could find out when he might be coming back.

Dani sniffed. Her steak! She turned it quickly and moaned on seeing the burnt underside of the quality cut of beef. Well, it was what she deserved, getting lost in thought about Thad! Dani sighed and shook her head.

She was sure Thad had Magnolia Bay's best interests in mind, but she was afraid it was her heart he'd stolen. . .and she had to get it back. Because, even if Thad returned to Magnolia Bay, it wouldn't be long before he went back to Dallas. She had to quit thinking about him. She saw no future to it—none at all.

She could do only one thing, and that was pray the Lord would help her get that Texas man out of her head.

★

By the end of the week Thad was already thinking about returning to Magnolia Bay, telling himself he needed to go back to work on the advertising campaign that was beginning to form in his mind. He truly liked the town and wanted to find the right hook to use to help the most.

He loved the town's slower pace. In a big city everything seemed to move too quickly. The days usually sped by, leaving him to wonder where they'd gone and why he hadn't enjoyed them more.

But there was always something he had to do, a project he had to check on, a place he had to be. He longed for a less hectic way of life. He wanted to spend time with people he cared about and to be more thankful for the ways the Lord had blessed him.

Cole was right. Thad had been to Magnolia Bay only a couple of times, and he felt its pull. Part of him was anxious to find a way to bring more people there so they could find out about it, and the other part wanted to keep its charm a secret. But keeping it a secret wasn't part of the job he'd taken. And he was having trouble coming up with anything that felt right. That being the case he needed to go back before long. He kept telling himself it was the town that drew him and a certain violet-eyed beauty who lived there had little to do with it; but somehow it didn't ring true.

seven

July turned to August, and Thad found himself watching the weather channel more than he had during the storms that swept through Dallas in the spring. But ever since his ride with Dani along the Mississippi Gulf Coast and her detailed explanations of what past hurricanes had done in the area, he'd had a new interest in the disturbances brewing in the Atlantic. Especially any that might affect his friends in Magnolia Bay. At the moment nothing seemed to pose a threat, and for that he was thankful.

He'd caught up on the work he needed to do in Dallas and could probably put together an advertising campaign for Magnolia Bay from here, but he wasn't happy with his ideas. They were good, but he was afraid they would bring too many tourists into Magnolia Bay—and he wasn't sure that was best for the town he'd come to love.

In fact he'd been thinking a lot about moving there, as Cole had done. He could conduct his business from almost anywhere. And with Linda engaged it was only a matter of time after she married before he'd have to look for another secretary. He wouldn't be upsetting other employees because at present his company consisted of him and Linda.

He'd worked for larger firms before branching out on his own, but he had no interest in becoming like them. He made a good living and could increase that if he took on additional jobs and hired others to do part of the work, but that wasn't what he wanted. This way he took on what he could manage, put his all into each job, and continued to love what he was doing.

With that in mind he decided he needed at least one more trip there—maybe more. Maybe it *was* time for a change. He hadn't been happy in Dallas since Meagan and then Cole had left. He still had friends here and loved his church, but it wasn't the same. He didn't want to make a rash decision, though. He needed to spend more time in Magnolia Bay to be sure it was right. Thad picked up the phone and dialed Bay Inn's number.

"Bay Inn, how may I help you?"

He recognized Ronni's voice. "Hi, Ronni. It's Thad. How are things there?"

"Everything is going well. When are you coming back to see us?"

"As a matter of fact I was calling to let that husband of yours know I need a place to stay again and see if you have a room open."

Ronni chuckled. "I can tell you what Cole would have said if he'd answered the phone. We have a room ready and waiting for you anytime."

"Do you really? I was prepared to wait for a reservation, provided it wouldn't take too long. Otherwise I could pitch a tent on the grounds."

He heard her chuckle again. "No need for that. We have an extra room in the family quarters just for you."

"Are you sure, Ronni? I don't want to impose—"

"Thad Cameron, you are Cole's best friend. And you are doing us all a favor by helping to revive Magnolia Bay. There is no way you would be imposing. Cole was saying just last night that he wished you'd pay another visit."

"If you're sure, tell him I'll be in town a week from tomorrow."

"Good! We look forward to having you."

"Thank you, Ronni."

"No thanks needed, Thad. See you in about a week."

Thad hung up the phone and smiled. What a blessing to have good friends to visit and stay with. He looked forward to seeing them all. But, he had to admit, he looked forward most to seeing Dani again.

On impulse he picked up the phone again. He had her home number in his cell phone from calling to set a time for them to meet when he was in Magnolia Bay. He quickly punched in her number. One ring. Two. On the sixth ring her answering machine picked up, but not knowing what kind of message to leave he hung up. She was out, no doubt on a date with someone. She probably hadn't given him a thought since he'd left. Thad didn't care for either of those ideas. But they were more than likely fact, and he should quit thinking about her.

No matter how many times he'd told himself to stop, though, he knew he couldn't—at least not until he saw her again and convinced himself her eyes weren't that soft shade of light purple.

❧

Dani watched the weather report on the small television in her office. A slight disturbance was brewing in the

Caribbean, but it looked as if it would be going into Mexico, south of Brownsville, Texas. She hoped it wouldn't grow in intensity.

So far it had been a mild summer, but that only caused Dani to worry more. It was doubtful they'd make it through this time of year without several storms reaching the Gulf of Mexico. And the farther into hurricane season they went, the more things would heat up. She wouldn't relax until after the end of November—no matter how much she'd like to. They had already had numerous emergency meetings, trying to prepare for the day warnings would go out for their area. But they all knew that no matter how prepared they were, they couldn't plan for some things. Oh, they'd probably come out all right with a category one or two as long as it didn't stay right over them or just offshore for hours or days. But a three or higher and it would be serious. Dani prayed off and on through each day for courage and wisdom to know what to do if a hurricane came to Magnolia Bay. She knew she could do nothing without the Lord's help.

When she wasn't watching, thinking, and praying about the weather, her thoughts were often on Thad. She wondered when he'd come back to Magnolia Bay to present his proposal to the city council. She kept telling herself she was silly for missing him—that she hadn't even known him that long—but nothing she said to herself seemed to work. She couldn't get him out of her mind.

Much as she'd like to find out when he might be coming back, she didn't want anyone to guess how much she wanted to know, so she just kept her ears open and hoped someone would volunteer the information.

She looked at her watch and decided to call it a day. They seemed to be getting longer all the time. She'd just grabbed her purse and was on her way out the door when her cell phone rang.

"Dani, it's Meagan. Hope I didn't catch you in the middle of anything."

"No, I'm just leaving work."

"Now?"

Dani chuckled. "Well, I did work a little late today." She didn't add that she worked late many days.

"I guess a city manager's job is never finished, is it?"

"There is a lot to keep up with. What's going on?"

"Oh, yes. Back to why I called. Thad is coming this weekend, and Nick and I are having a cookout this Saturday. I wanted to see if you could make it."

At the sound of Thad's name her heart began an uneven beat. "Oh, that's nice, Meagan. I can't think of a reason why I wouldn't be able to. Do you need me to bring anything?"

"Just bring yourself. Come on over around six, and we'll eat whenever Nick says it's ready. He's grilling, and I'm sure Cole and Thad will supervise, so no telling when we'll eat."

"Ronni and Cole are coming too?"

"Yes, they'll be here along with Claudia and Mike and Alice too. And we've asked several more people to come. You will join us, won't you?"

That was good. There was safety in numbers, and maybe with all those people around she wouldn't give away how glad she'd be to see Thad. "I'll be there. Thank you, Meagan."

"We're looking forward to it. See you Saturday."

Dani dropped her cell phone in her purse and grinned all the way to her car. On the way home she told herself it would be good to do something other than housework and laundry on a Saturday night. She was getting tired of that. Mighty tired. But deep inside she knew it was Thad's return to Magnolia Bay that was responsible for the smile on her face. She would see him soon!

At home she made herself an omelet and sat out on her patio to eat it. A soft cooling breeze made it comfortable to be outside, and she loved the sweet smells in her garden. The only thing that would make it more pleasant would be to share her meal with someone. Content with her own company most of the time, she couldn't explain the recent pangs of loneliness she'd felt. She wasn't even sure when they first started.

Oh, she missed her parents; but they were in a better place now, and she'd grown accustomed to living alone. She'd never had a problem occupying her time and even less now that she was city manager. She loved to read, garden, and cook. She didn't mind cleaning house and had enjoyed redecorating in the last few months.

But what she longed for was someone to share all that with. Someone to share her life with, to cook for, to eat with, and to talk to at the end of the day. Dani didn't know why she suddenly felt she needed all of that now when she'd never given it much thought until a few—until Thad Cameron had stepped into her life.

Meeting him for breakfast, spending her days and even some evenings with him had shown her what was missing from her life. On the Fourth of July when she thought Thad was about to kiss her and then didn't, she'd been disappointed. But not until later had she realized how much she wanted him to kiss her even though she didn't want to admit it.

She had to put thoughts of that near kiss out of her mind. He hadn't carried through with it, and besides, what good would it do? Dani sighed and picked up her plate. She hadn't heard from him since he'd left town, and even though he was coming back it wasn't because of her. She had to get him out of her mind. Dani shook her head as she entered her kitchen. She was finding that part much easier said than done.

❧

On Saturday morning Thad took a deep breath of gulf air as he drove along Bay Drive. This was it. The place he wanted to call home.

He wasn't ready to tell anyone yet, but he was sure it was what he wanted. It seemed like home here, and he'd felt he belonged as he was welcomed back to Bay Inn by Miss Claudia and the Bannisters the night before. Cole had showed him to one of the guest rooms in the family apartment on the third floor. It had a balcony overlooking the walking trail down to the bay. The grounds were lush with hydrangeas and roses in full bloom.

He'd joined Miss Claudia and the Bannisters and their other guests for dinner in the downstairs dining room, and Thad watched as Miss Claudia gave each guest her undivided attention at intervals throughout the meal. He could see why the inn stayed full.

It wasn't until they went back upstairs and had coffee and dessert in the family quarters that talk had turned to Magnolia Bay.

"Have you decided what kind of ad will work for us?" Miss Claudia had asked.

Thad shook his head. "Not completely. I have several ideas, but I'm not sure they're the best ones. Before I present anything to the city council, I want to think it's right."

"Well, you're welcome to stay as long as you need to," Cole said. "You know that."

"I do. And I really appreciate it. It's a good feeling to know I'm welcome."

"Anytime. I wish you'd just go ahead and move here. Magnolia Bay could use a new business or two operating out of here."

"That's right. We need a bigger tax base. We aren't just after tourists, you know," Miss Claudia said.

Thad had been tempted to tell them he was thinking of doing that but held back. He wanted to make sure before he said anything to anyone.

Now as he drove around town he was on the lookout for FOR SALE signs. He'd already passed several older homes he'd like to see inside, but he'd talk to Cole first. He wasn't sure if he wanted to buy an older home or have one built. Either way, though, he'd want Cole's input. He could help with renovations on an older home if they were needed or draw up plans for a new one.

Thad wished it were a weekday so he could drop by Dani's office. She'd been in the back of his mind ever since he'd arrived in town. He thought about driving by her house but wasn't sure what he'd say. Would he go up to her door and tell her he wanted to see how purple her eyes were? No. He couldn't tell her they reminded him of lilacs and violets and all kinds of flowers and he thought he could spend the rest of his life trying to decide what shade they were—not yet anyway.

He'd wait until he ran into her. Surely he'd see her at church tomorrow, if not before. He was hoping she would be at Nick and Meagan's tonight. When Nick and Meagan had called to tell him they were having a cookout while he was in town, he didn't want to sound as if his coming depended on who else was there, so he hadn't asked about the guest list. He did know Miss Claudia and Cole and Ronni were going. He'd have a good time. It would just be better if Dani was there.

❧

Dani changed clothes four times before she finally decided on white capris and a lilac-colored shirt. Meagan had said to dress comfortably since they'd mostly be outdoors, but Dani didn't want to go too casual. She kept telling herself it was only a night out with friends. Still, her fingertips shook as she fastened the back of her earrings, and she knew it was because Thad would be there. She put on a silver necklace and a bracelet to match the earrings and slipped into lilac-colored sandals. This was one of her favorite outfits. At least she felt confident she looked her best, even if she was a bundle of nerves.

By the time she'd driven over to Nick and Meagan's she thought she'd convinced herself to relax—or at least she hoped she appeared to be. Meagan answered the door and led her out back to where most of their guests were already assembled.

Dani answered everyone's greetings with a cheery hello and tried to appear nonchalant as she spotted Thad coming toward her.

"Dani. It's good to see you. I hope you were able to catch up on your work?"

"I was." *But I wouldn't have minded getting even more behind if you'd stayed longer.* Her heart pounded so loud she was afraid he could hear it. She couldn't believe how good it was to see him again.

"I felt bad that I took up so much of your time. I'm glad you were able to catch up."

"It wasn't a problem." *I didn't have anything else to do after you left.* "How are plans going for your advertising campaign?"

"Well, I still don't have a handle on it. I'm hoping this trip will solidify several ideas I have."

"You'll be available to show Thad around some more, if he needs you to, won't you, Dani?" Claudia asked from over her shoulder, reminding Dani that her relationship with Thad was a business one for the good of the city. And that was why he was here. *Not* to see her. But she knew that already. At least her brain did. The problem was getting her pounding heart to accept it.

"Certainly." Dani was thankful for the reminder. She needed it. The way her pulse raced at his nearness had her thinking along an entirely different vein.

"That's good to know. Thank you, Dani," Thad said as

Meagan called them all to the large table set up under the trees.

Dani found herself seated between Thad and Claudia. If not for the recent reminder that they were business acquaintances, she could have begun to think they were on a date. He was so attentive to her, making sure she had some of everything on her plate and her iced tea glass was full. Of course he did the same for Claudia, but Dani couldn't keep from wishing it were a date.

Talk turned to the advertising campaign when Mike asked Thad how it was going.

"Not as well as I'd hoped it would be by now. I'm having a little trouble deciding what direction to take. That's one reason I'm here now."

"I can see how it would require a lot of thought. Selling a town can't be easy. Especially since we aren't trying to draw people in to gamble their savings away," Cole said. "We're trying to attract a special kind of tourist."

"Since we aren't letting the casinos in our city limits I don't see how we can help but draw tourists who want to enjoy the Southern charm and small-town feel here," Nick said. "At least that's what Meagan and I would like to see."

Alice nodded. "Mike and I feel the same way."

"I think that's what we all are hoping for," Claudia said.

"Obviously those tourists are out there—Bay Inn is attracting them," Thad said.

"Well, yes, but not totally," Ronni said. "Sadly some of our guests have found their way to the casinos too. They just seem to like spending the rest of their time in a quieter atmosphere."

"Are you sure you want to target tourists?" Thad asked.

Everyone at the table was quiet, and Dani held her breath. Did Thad see things the way she did?

"What do you mean?" Mike asked.

"It sounds as if you don't want Magnolia Bay turning into a spring break kind of place or a town known for its lively night life."

"Exactly," Mike said.

"You've got that right," Nick agreed. "Do you have an idea of how we can keep that from happening?"

Thad shrugged and shook his head. "I think we might need to change directions, but I don't have anything concrete yet."

"Well, take all the time you need," Cole said. "We want this done right."

Dani's heart flooded with joy. But it wasn't just because it sounded as if Thad and all these new friends of hers felt the same way she did about Magnolia Bay. He was going to be here awhile. And hard as she tried to tell herself she shouldn't care, she knew it was a losing battle. She already did.

eight

Thad joined Cole for a jog when they got home from the Chambers home. He felt better about the ad campaign. These people didn't want Magnolia Bay to turn into only a tourist town. To his great relief they wanted something better. So did he. He just had to come up with the right idea.

"Feels like old times," Cole said as they rounded the bend for the third time and started back toward the inn.

"It does, doesn't it?"

"Why don't you move on over here? If I could relocate my business, so can you."

"You had an ulterior motive in all that. Ronni was here." *So is Dani.* Thad tried to push that thought out of his mind. Although she'd been very sweet tonight she hadn't exactly welcomed him with open arms as the rest of the group had, and she'd been quiet while they were talking about the advertising campaign.

"I'm sure there's a woman here for you. I even have one in mind."

"Oh? Who is it?"

"Dani Phillips would be a great catch."

Thad's heart thudded in his chest at her name. *That she would.* "Dani isn't interested in me that way."

"I notice you didn't say *you* weren't interested in *her*."

82

"You're entirely too observant for my own good," Thad said with a chuckle.

"Ah-ha. So you *are* interested in her?"

Cole was his best friend, and they'd shared a lot. He could be truthful with him. "Lot of good it will do me. She thinks of me as part of her job."

"How do you know that?"

"You didn't notice her jumping with joy to see me again, did you?"

"Well, no, but that doesn't mean anything. Women hide their true feelings sometimes."

"What made you so wise?" Thad asked.

Cole laughed. "Ronni."

"I see. Well, I'm not sure I'm ready to get on that. . .roller coaster. . .again anyway." Thad was beginning to feel a bit winded.

"You're over Meagan."

Thad nodded. "I know."

"You are. . .no coward, Thad." Cole sounded a little out of breath too. "I think you and Dani. . .would make a great couple. But you'll have to put a toe. . .in the water to find out."

"Hmm."

"And. . .take it from. . .me. It's hard to carry on. . .a long-distance romance."

"I'm sure. . .it is." Thad wouldn't want to anyway.

"It'd sure. . .be a lot easier. . .if you'd move here."

"I'll think. . .about it."

"Good," Cole said. "That's what. . .I wanted to hear."

They arrived back at the inn and cooled down at a

slower pace before dropping onto two lounge chairs. It was a couple of minutes before either of them spoke again.

"I don't jog. . .as much as I used to," Cole said. "Ronni and I. . .jogged a little right before and after we got married, but things got so busy around here we let it slide."

"Obviously I haven't been. . .keeping up with it, either." Thad chuckled, still breathing hard.

"Maybe if you move here. . .we could both get in better shape?" Cole grinned at him.

"Maybe."

Thad was still chuckling when he got ready for bed later. It would be good to live around his best friend again. He'd almost told Cole he was ready to look for a place, but he knew he needed to be sure. He didn't want to get his friend's hopes up and then change his mind.

He stepped onto the balcony and looked out into the night. The stars sparkled in the clear night sky, and the moon shone brightly, kissing the leaves of the trees around him. Moving here was something he had to consider a lot. His instincts told him to make the move, but thinking about Dani gave him second thoughts. He would like to pursue a relationship with her. She intrigued him in a way no woman ever had. Not even Meagan.

She was lovely, and those eyes were purple, although he still wasn't sure what shade to call them. They seemed to change each time he saw her. But besides being so pretty she was genuinely nice, intelligent, and courageous— she'd have to be to take on managing a town that was fighting for survival. That she loved Magnolia Bay was obvious. And he had a feeling that if she ever gave her heart to someone it would be forever. The way his heart had thudded in his chest the moment he'd seen her tonight made him realize he'd like to be that someone. And while he thought he wanted to live here from now on, he was pretty sure he wanted to share the rest of his life—anywhere—with Dani.

And that might not be possible. She might not be interested in him. Could he live here under those circumstances? Why not? He had to live somewhere. After Meagan chose Nick over him, the hurt was there, even in Dallas. Would it have been worse if they'd lived in the same town? Thad didn't know. What he did know was the Lord wouldn't give him more than he could bear, and if He'd healed his heart from Meagan's rejection, He could do it again if necessary.

Cole was right. He had to dip his toe in the water. That was the only way to find out if it was hot or cold, if he could swim or not, if he stood a chance with Dani or not. He wasn't a coward. And he'd never know if Dani could care for him if he didn't try to find out.

It was time to pray and let the Lord lead him in making a decision.

ße

Dani laid out what she was going to wear to church the next day, wondering if Thad would be at church. She hoped so. Over and over she'd told herself she was being silly. But she couldn't help it. She felt like a teenager experiencing her first crush.

Jimmy Mathews. Yes, that was his name. My, she hadn't thought of him in years. He was her first love. . .actually her only real crush. Her mom had passed away her sophomore year, and after that she hadn't had time for crushes anymore. But because of Jimmy Mathews she'd never forget her freshman year.

She couldn't wait to get to school each day, to hear his voice, to see his smile—which she'd convinced herself was meant only for her. The ninth-grade banquet had come, and she'd hoped with everything in her that he would ask her to go with him, but her heart had been broken when he'd asked someone else to go.

Dani sighed. If he'd actually acted interested in her, shy as she was, she didn't know what she would have done, but he sure livened up her ninth-grade year.

Now here she was at thirty, feeling not much different from how she did back then. She couldn't wait to see Thad, to hear his voice, to see his smile. Chances were that her heart would be broken again, but it would hurt much more this time. The man had given her no cause to think he cared for her. But try as she might she couldn't seem to keep her heart from beating faster, her tummy from doing somersaults, or her pulse from racing each time he was near. And she wasn't sure she wanted to—wasn't sure of anything except that she didn't seem to have control of her heart.

She watched the late news before turning in. The last storm had indeed hit Mexico, but she still couldn't breathe easy. She wasn't pleased to see that several tropical storms were forming. One out in the Atlantic looked as if it might stay there, moving north and not a threat to anyone, but the other one had formed in the Caribbean. Several of the early forecasts had it eventually going into the Gulf of Mexico. Once there it could end up anywhere. She prayed it wouldn't intensify and, as always, that if it came their way the Lord would guide her in helping her town get through it.

The next morning she checked again before leaving for church. It had become a hurricane overnight but was still a category one. She prayed all the way across town, as she drove to her church, that the storm would dissipate and do no harm.

Reminding herself she could do nothing about it for the moment, Dani prayed, asking the Lord to help her count her blessings and not worry so much. *He* was in control, and He would be there for those in the path of the storms.

Her spirits lifted as she walked toward church. She was pleased to see Thad was with Cole and Ronni in the "Thirties" Sunday school class, along with Meagan and Nick. They'd been studying Psalms, and the verse today seemed appropriate for this time of year. The Lord was truly reminding her to take her worries to Him, for Psalm 46:1 said, "God is our refuge and strength, an ever-present help in trouble."

Dani felt as if a load had been lifted off her shoulders. The Lord would be with her and her town as He always had been.

It seemed natural to sit on the same pew with the others for church services. She wasn't sure how she and Thad ended up sitting beside each other, but she wouldn't complain. He had a beautiful tenor voice, and shivers ran down Dani's spine as the people around her raised their voices in song and praise to the Lord. The sermon was an encouraging one, and when the service came to an end she felt lifted up and ready to start a new week.

"We're going to the Seaside Surf and Turf for lunch," Nick said. "Why don't you all join us?"

"I'd like that," Thad said. "How about you, Dani? Want to ride with me?"

For a moment Dani couldn't find her voice. He'd asked her to go with him.

"I can bring you back to pick up your car later or follow you home and take you back."

That was an offer she wasn't going to turn down. She nodded. "I'd like that. Why don't you follow me to my house and I'll ride with you?"

"We'll go ahead and get a table then," Cole said. "See you there."

଺

Thad hoped Dani hadn't seen the thumbs-up Cole gave him as he followed her out of the building. Cole was probably patting himself on the shoulder thinking Thad was taking his advice in dipping his toe in the water. And maybe he should, but Thad thought he would have invited her even if he and Cole hadn't talked about it the night before.

They walked out in a group, and Thad found Dani was parked close to him. "I'll follow you to your house, all right?"

"That's fine," Dani said.

By the time he reached his car she had pulled out of her parking space and was waiting for him. It took only a few minutes to reach her place. It was a charming cottage in the older part of town, and it was apparent that she took great care of it. Painted white with dark green trim and shutters, it looked fresh and welcoming. He wished they had time for him to see what it looked like on the inside, but with the others waiting for them Dani parked her car and hurried over to his. He only had time to lean over and open the door for her.

"It's a beautiful day, isn't it?" he asked as she slipped into the passenger seat.

"It is. It's going to be very warm, though. Is it this hot in Dallas?"

"Oh, it can be unbearable in Dallas in the summer. And we don't have the gentle wind off the bay as you do. I like that cooling breeze."

"It does help a lot. And we have a light breeze most days. But some days are just plain still and heavy with humidity. You haven't experienced those yet."

"No, but I'd find it hard to believe they could be any worse than Dallas can be this time of year."

They pulled into the parking lot of the restaurant, and Thad hurried around to open her door. She did look lovely today, her short hair curling away from her face and ruffling in the breeze. In the sunshine her eyes were lighter, reminding him of the lilacs his grandmother had loved to grow.

"Thank you," she said as she got out of the car.

"You're welcome." Something about opening a door for a woman or pulling out a chair made a man feel chivalrous. One didn't get to do it often in this day and age. Most women had opened the door or taken their own seat before a man could do it for them. And then maybe it was because a lot of men had never been taught those particular manners and left women to their own devices. And that was too bad, because somehow doing those small things made him feel. . .manlier.

Cole must have told the receptionist they were expected because they were sent to the back dining room where the rest of the group was already looking at menus. Thad pulled out a chair for Dani and tried to ignore the smug grin Cole flashed him. Subtleness was not one of his friend's strengths. Thad would have to talk with him.

When the waitress came to them Dani ordered the butterfly shrimp, and he chose the New York strip steak. After she left to put in their orders, the conversation turned to the weather.

"Do you have the latest update, Dani?" Meagan asked.

"I haven't seen anything since this morning. Last I heard there's a good chance it's going into the Gulf of Mexico."

"We've been blessed so far this year. It's been pretty quiet," Ronni said. "I guess it's too much to hope it will stay that way."

"Well, you know they've been predicting more and bigger storms for the next few years. I'd like to think they're wrong, but I'm sure the people in Pensacola would be the first to agree with that prediction," Nick said. "I had some business there last week, and they are still dealing with blue roofs."

"Blue roofs?" Thad wasn't sure what they were talking about.

"They're temporary tarp-like roofs," Cole said. "They're supposed to be good for only about six months or so—just until a new roof can be put up. But so many homes were damaged after the storms they've had the last few years, they've never caught up."

"I pray they don't get hit this year," Ronni said. "They've had more than their share of heartache."

"And I pray we don't either," Alice added. "I don't want *anyone* to get hit."

"No one does," Meagan said.

"The hardest part is when a storm gets into the gulf and you know it's going to hit somewhere," Cole said. "Rarely do they make an about-face and go back out."

Thad could feel the tension building around the table at Cole's words. Hurricane season was no laughing matter for these people. "I feel bad. I know they've come ashore in Texas, and Galveston Island is vulnerable. But living in Dallas, where the most we get from one is a lot of rain—which is usually needed at this time of year—I've not paid much attention to them until now."

"We've found most people who aren't directly affected by them don't pay that much attention. I only did because I had relatives here," Cole said.

"Me too," Meagan agreed. "I guess it's just human nature to concern ourselves with only what directly affects us or our loved ones."

"I have a lot of people I care about right here." Thad said. "I think I'll be watching the tropical update more often now."

nine

When Thad brought her back to her house Dani shocked herself by asking him in for a glass of iced tea. She was pleased when he didn't hesitate to say yes.

"I love this area of Magnolia Bay," he said as she unlocked her front door. "It's such a mixture of grand old homes and—"

"And smaller cottages like mine."

"It's lovely, Dani," he said as he looked around her living room.

"I love it. It's small, compared to some of the others on the block. It has this room, which would have been called the parlor when it was first built, a dining room and the kitchen downstairs, and three bedrooms and two baths upstairs. Daddy installed the second bathroom for me."

"They made rooms larger than they do now, though. It's a nice size."

"It is." She turned the television on. "Let me check the weather, and then we'll have our tea."

Thad watched as the tropical update came on. He could feel Dani relax with the news that the storm had weakened and looked as if it would hit a barely populated area of Texas.

"Good news," Thad said.

"Yes, for the time being. Another one's coming off the African coast, though."

"That's pretty far out yet to predict what it will do, isn't it?"

"Yes. We should have a few days before we have to watch it closely."

"Good." Thad thought he might be almost as relieved as she was.

"Come on back," she said, turning the television off and leading the way to her kitchen. It had been updated several years earlier, and she loved it. "This is my favorite room."

"I can see why."

It was large enough to have a small round table in a bay window off to the side and had plenty of cabinet space and a walk-in pantry. Her appliances were new, made to look old, as if they were original to the house, and she had a center island she used everyday.

She filled two tall glasses with ice and tea and handed one to Thad. "We can have it here or out in my garden. It's usually nice even in the middle of the day."

"Let's go outside."

Putting the pitcher and her glass on a tray, she led the way outside. "Okay. Follow me."

Dani enjoyed showing off her garden. Crepe myrtles bloomed in several places in the yard, and a huge magnolia tree took center stage. She hated the leaves that fell but loved the blossoms. She had planted azaleas, hydrangeas, and gardenias around trees and along the perimeter of her lot with annuals added here and there all over the yard for extra color during the hot months.

In the middle of the garden under the magnolia tree was a small wrought iron table and two chairs. "Let's sit here in the shade."

Thad dropped down into the chair across from her. "I believe your garden is even more lush and sweet smelling than the grounds at Bay Inn, Dani."

"Thank you. That's quite a compliment. I love the gardens at Bay Inn. They do have more room to spread out, though. Sometimes I think I have way too much planted here, but I like it all and don't want to get rid of any of it, so I guess it doesn't matter."

Thad looked around and then back into her eyes. "I wouldn't change a thing."

They listened to the birds singing and watched and laughed as two squirrels chased each other up and around the branches of the magnolia tree until they tired of the game and jumped to another tree. Dani was surprised at how comfortable she felt with the silence between them. She felt no need to fill the quiet with chatter, and evidently neither did Thad. Dani filled their glasses several times before she emptied the pitcher. The shadows were lengthening when they finished their tea.

"I guess I'd better be getting back to the inn." Thad drained his glass and stood up.

"You can go out here at the side gate." Dani led him to the side of the house where a wrought iron gate opened to the driveway. "Cole will be out looking for you if you don't get back there soon."

Thad laughed. "I don't think so. You should have seen us last night. We went jogging and found out neither of us had kept at it since he moved back here. He says he jogged for a while when he came, but after he and Ronni got married they stopped."

"I guess they stay pretty busy, Cole with his contracting company and Ronni running the inn."

Thad nodded. "I think so. But they don't seem to mind. They're just happy to be together."

"I'm glad. Ronni deserves someone who loves her the way Cole does. They do seem very happy together."

"They are. So are Meagan and Nick. I'm glad for them too." Thad inclined his head and smiled. "I was almost engaged to her. Did you know that?"

Dani shrugged. "I'd heard something about it."

He nodded and smiled. It was a small town after all. "I'm sure you did. But, once I saw her and Nick together, I knew it wasn't meant to be between the two of us. It was obvious she hadn't gotten over him and that he was in love with her. They make a good couple."

"They do." She smiled. "Meagan told me they give you the credit for getting them back together."

"I don't know about that, but I did step out of the way and nudge them both to recognize their feelings for each other."

"Obviously it worked."

"It did. And I'm glad." He turned back at his car. "Thanks for going with me today and for asking me to stay awhile. I enjoyed it."

"So did I," Dani admitted softly.

"I'll see you in the next day or two. I may have more questions for you."

"I'll be in my office."

Thad nodded as he got into his car. "Bye."

"Bye." She glanced at her watch. If she hurried, she

could make it to the evening service. She usually went and was glad she had a place to go tonight. Suddenly the thought of being by herself this evening made her feel more lonely than usual.

❧

Thad could have kicked himself when he saw Dani enter the church about fifteen minutes after he did. He could have asked her to come with him. But spending the afternoon with her, in her backyard, he'd lost track of time and even forgot what day it was until he neared the church.

Now he hurried over to sit beside her before the service started. She looked a little surprised when he slipped into the pew beside her.

"Dani, I forgot what night it was until I nearly passed the church. I would have asked you to come with me otherwise."

"It's okay."

"How about meeting at Beach Burgers after the service? I'll treat."

"You don't have to do that," Dani said.

"I know. But I'd sure like your company if you don't have any other plans."

Her smile gave him hope.

"I haven't had a Beach Burger in a while. I'd love to meet you there."

Thad was glad the song leader stood up to lead the opening hymn because he suddenly felt like singing. Her sweet alto joined his tenor, and they sang in harmony. Thad sent up a silent prayer of thankfulness that she wasn't upset he hadn't asked her to come to church and seemed to understand he'd forgotten it was Sunday night. What she didn't know was that it was thoughts of her that had his mind so busy he could think of little else. Like how good it had felt to sit in her garden and listen to the afternoon go by and how comfortable he felt in her company. Or how beautiful she looked today and that he finally knew he would never pin down the color of her eyes. They changed from light to dark depending on the time of day, the color she wore, and even her mood. But they were always beautiful.

Dani turned the page of the songbook, making him realize he'd been singing on auto pilot, and he sent up another silent prayer for forgiveness for letting his mind wander from the service. It took effort, especially with Dani beside him, but for the next hour he concentrated on what he was there for—worshiping the Lord. And, while he couldn't ignore the woman at his side, he was able to focus on the lesson and enjoy being there with her.

When they left church Thad followed Dani to Beach Burgers. It was still light out, but the setting sun sparkled on the bay, coloring it with orange and magenta. As he and Dani waited on their burgers they watched the water lapping at the shore and talked about anything that came to mind. That was another thing that drew him to this woman. He was comfortable with her whether they were talking or silent. It didn't matter.

He enjoyed sharing this meal with her even more than the one the night before or lunch at noon today. Eating here was something he'd done only with Dani, and memories of their lunches here had been special to him during the past few weeks while he was in Dallas. He had a feeling he was falling deeply for this woman and couldn't seem to do anything about it.

He hated for the day to end. It had been one of the most pleasant he could remember. But nothing lasted forever. As they finished their supper the sun set and the sky darkened, bringing the day to a close.

Thad walked Dani to her car. He didn't want to leave her without making some kind of plan to see her again. "Want to meet for breakfast in the morning?"

She turned from unlocking her car door. "Do you need me to show you around some more?"

"Not really. I just thought it'd be nice to start the day with breakfast at the diner."

She paused for a moment before answering, and he was afraid she was going to turn him down. But she didn't. "It would. What time?"

"How about nine?"

"That should work. I have an emergency preparedness meeting at eight. It should be over by then."

"I'll get us a table." He looked down at her and met her gaze. He'd never get tired of looking into her eyes or at her lips. He was about to lower his head to find out how soft those lips were when she slipped into her car. Thad sighed inwardly. Would he ever find out what it was like to kiss her?

"See you in the morning, Thad."

" 'Night, Dani."

He watched her drive away before he slid into his car. He sure hoped his timing improved one of these days.

❧

Dani showered and prepared for bed humming to herself. She couldn't remember a day or an evening she'd enjoyed more. Spending the whole day with Thad was like a dream come true for her, and it was something she could easily get used to.

She didn't know if it was wishful thinking or not, but for a minute she thought he might kiss her. He'd looked at her so intently that her heart had beat triple time, but then the moment had passed; afraid he would think she was expecting him to kiss her, she'd quickly slid into her car. What if she'd waited one more minute? Would he have kissed her? Dani sighed and shook her head. One day she would have to quit second-guessing him and see what he intended to do.

She turned on the TV to the weather report. The storm off Africa was moving slowly. For now there was no telling where it would go. Dani felt she could relax for a few days more and sighed with relief and thankfulness.

Dani clicked off the remote and bowed her head. The Lord had blessed her with a wonderful day today, and she thanked Him for it. She also asked Him to watch over everyone along the Gulf Coast and anywhere else that might be threatened during this hurricane season.

ten

The meeting ran long with all parties concerned that the storm in the Atlantic was strengthening and had picked up speed overnight. While they were in no imminent danger it seemed to be moving due west, and if it kept the same track and speed it would be in the Caribbean in a few days. In the meantime they wanted to make sure all the city services were ready just in case. Police, fire and rescue, and the other emergency services were well represented.

Since she'd gone in early to make up for the time she was taking off to meet Thad, she didn't feel guilty for leaving the office. It was a little after nine when she reached the coffee shop. She spotted him right away, back in the booth they'd always managed to sit in when he was here. He didn't seem too concerned that she was late—in fact he was looking over a newspaper and only glanced up when she slipped into the seat opposite him.

"Hi! I'm glad you made it." He folded up the paper and smiled at her. "Did your meeting run long?"

Evidently he wasn't quite as oblivious to the time as she first thought. "A little. But we all feel better knowing we're about as prepared as we can get."

"I noticed the storm out there is getting bigger."

"It is. But we have a few more days before we have to worry too much about it."

"Good. Let's hope it weakens. I'm sure you're busy this time of year. Thanks for taking the time to join me for breakfast."

Lori, the waitress who'd served them before, came to their table with a cup of coffee for Dani and a pot to refill Thad's cup. "It's good to see you both again. What are you having today?"

"I want the hungry man's breakfast," Thad said with a grin.

"Whoa! You must be starving," Dani said, knowing that breakfast was huge. It consisted of eggs, pancakes, bacon, sausage, ham, and hash browns—with gravy and biscuits on the side.

Thad grinned at her. "Cole woke me up early to go jogging this morning. I am kind of hungry. Besides, I wanted to try it last time I was here and never did. I'm going for it today."

"Ahh, I see." Dani smiled at the waitress. "Well, I've been sitting down for the last hour. I think I'll just have an omelet and toast, please."

"Coming right up—I have to see if he can eat all of this breakfast." Lori grinned as she left to turn in their order.

"Worked up an appetite, did you?" Dani asked before taking a sip of coffee.

Thad chuckled. "I did."

"What are your plans for the day?"

"I'm going to walk around town, visit some of the people I met last time, and let the atmosphere sink in. And hope the right idea comes to me."

"Sounds like a plan. It must be hard to keep that small-town feel back in Dallas."

He didn't tell her the hardest part of being in Dallas was keeping her off his mind. "It was difficult being there after the peacefulness of Magnolia Bay. I know some people thrive on city life, but I've found I like a slower pace and getting to know people better."

Dani gazed out the window at the bay across the street. She shook her head and looked back at Thad. "I can't imagine living in a big city. I don't much like the traffic on the occasions when I've gone up to Jackson or over to New Orleans. I usually can't wait to get home. I went to college in Hattiesburg, and it wasn't too bad, although it was still a little big to me."

"I doubt you'd be happy in Dallas then."

Dani sighed. "You're probably right. Guess I was just small-town born and bred."

"There's nothing wrong with that. And maybe that's what I like so much about Magnolia Bay. Some of my best memories are of visiting my grandparents on their farm about fifty miles from Dallas. I liked the small town they went to for shopping and church. But even it's not so little anymore and has lost some of its charm."

"I hope that doesn't happen to Magnolia Bay. With all this advertising the city council wants to do—"

"Dani, I'm going to try to come up with something that won't hurt this town. I don't want it changed either."

Sudden tears formed behind her eyes, and she was afraid that if she spoke she wouldn't be able to keep them from spilling over. So she nodded and was thankful the waitress returned with their breakfasts, saving her from having to talk to Thad just then.

"Here you go," Lori said as she placed Thad's humongous breakfast in front of him. Then she put Dani's much smaller one on the table.

Thad looked at his plate a moment and then chuckled. "You weren't kidding, were you? This is an awful lot of food."

"Now you just remember what your mama always told you. Clean your plate." With that Lori laughed and left the table.

"I don't know where to start," Thad said, his fork in midair.

"And I don't know what to tell you. I think I'd go with the eggs so they don't get cold."

He nodded and took a bite of egg. "Good thinking."

After that they didn't talk for the next few minutes as Thad tried to make a dent in the food on his plate. Dani was finished long before him, but she enjoyed sipping her coffee and watching him go at it. She wondered what it would be like to share breakfast with him every morning.

"Want a piece of sausage?" he asked Dani.

She grinned and shook her head. "No, thank you."

"Come on, Dani. I don't want to leave anything on this platter. I know that's what our waitress expects, but she was right. Mom did always tell me to clean my plate. Help me out here. Please."

Dani laughed. When he looked at her that way, though, her heart did a funny twist, and she knew she couldn't refuse his request. She glanced at his plate. "Oh, all right. One piece of sausage and maybe a spoonful of hash browns. You'll have to eat the rest yourself."

"Every little bit helps. Thank you." He slid a sausage onto her plate and spooned some hash browns on while she was sampling the sausage.

"You're welcome." The sausage did taste good. And she had a weakness for hash browns.

Thad managed to eat the rest, and Dani had to tease him. "Okay, we're meeting at Beach Burgers for lunch, right? What time?"

The look on Thad's face was priceless. "You're kidding, right?"

"Would I do that?"

"I certainly hope so. There's no way I'll be able to eat another thing until tonight. But how about we go to the Seaside Surf and Turf?"

Dani felt bad. She didn't want him to think she expected him to eat all his meals with her. "I *was* just teasing, Thad. Please don't feel you have to ask me to dinner."

"I know I don't have to, Dani." His gaze was steady as he looked at her. "But I really want you to go with me. I feel a little out of place at the inn. I'm not a paying guest, and I don't want Miss Claudia and the Bannisters to think they have to entertain me when they have all those guests to see to."

Was he only wanting her to go because he felt uncomfortable? If that was the case—

"Dani, I can't think of anyone I'd rather have dinner with. Please say you'll go with me."

It wasn't the case. He wanted to be with her. Dani's heart seemed to swoop down to her tummy as his gaze never wavered from hers. "Yes, of course I'll go. Thank you for the invitation."

"What time will be best for you? Would seven be all right?"

"Seven will be fine." Anytime would be fine with her. Anytime at all.

"Good. I'll pick you up then."

Lori brought their bill, and her mouth fell open when she looked at Thad's empty plate. "I can't believe you ate it all. I've never seen anyone able to eat the whole thing."

Dani looked at Thad and raised her eyebrow.

"Aw, I have to confess. Dani helped me out a little."

"Uh-huh. I knew you couldn't do it," Lori said smugly.

Dani rushed to Thad's defense. "Oh, he'd have done it. All I ate was one sausage and a couple of spoonfuls of hash browns. He could have finished that easily enough."

"Oh, I don't know about that," he admitted. "But it sure was a challenge to clean that plate."

"I think it was meant to be," Lori said as she took their empty dishes away.

"I guess I have to let you get back to work now," Thad said, drinking a last sip of coffee before sliding out of his seat. "Thank you for taking time out of your day. . .and for helping me clean my plate."

"You're welcome. Thank you for breakfast."

"Anytime." He paid for their meals, and they walked outside. "See you tonight."

"See you then."

⁂

Thad watched Dani as she headed down the street toward the city offices. She waved at several people who called out her name and bent down to talk to a small child in a stroller when the mother stopped to talk to Dani.

She was one special woman, and Thad was already looking forward to the evening when he'd see her again. Spending time with Dani Phillips was proving to be habit-forming.

He spent the rest of the day walking around town, talking to some of the same store owners and city residents he had the last time. They greeted him as if he were one of their own, and again he was impressed by how friendly they were.

He especially liked visiting with Brad and Lydia Waters at their flower shop. They treated him like an old friend.

"Thad Cameron! It's good to see you again," Brad said. "Have you come back with a plan for our town?"

"I'm still working on it, Brad. Right now I'm in the listening mode. You have any ideas for me?"

"I've heard a lot of good things about you. I don't think you need my help. But, now that you ask, I'd like to see us draw more people to *live* here. As a general rule we don't get much business from tourists here at the flower shop."

"That's right," Lydia agreed. "But some people are bound to be working along the coast and would like to get away from the touristy atmosphere when they go home from work. We have a lot of real estate for sale here from people moving out. What we really need is to bring people in to stay."

"I noticed a number of homes for sale in the newspaper." He'd spotted several homes he wouldn't mind looking at later on. From the sound of it, it was a buyers' market—at least for now. But once attention was drawn back to the town it wouldn't stay that way. He had only a limited time frame to find a home if he was going to move.

"Well, from what I've been hearing, the city council is thinking about trying to get some computer-oriented industry in here. That sure would solve a lot of our problems," Brad said. "They're probably counting on your campaign to bring attention to Magnolia Bay so that some of the companies will open a plant near here."

This was news to Thad, but perhaps his and his friends' wishes for this town were shared by the city council too. He needed to talk to Miss Claudia or request a meeting with the council. If they were all on the same page with what they wanted for Magnolia Bay, it would make his job easier.

"That would be a more permanent way to bring people into town. Tourists are good, and the town could still benefit from them. . .maybe those who would be interested in the historical aspect of the town. . .and the peace and quiet." New ideas were flying around in his head, and Thad felt as if he were on the verge of coming up with an idea that was just right for Magnolia Bay.

He was right in thinking he'd needed to come back there to work it out. When he left the flower shop he punched Miss Claudia's phone number into his cell phone and requested a meeting with her and the other members of the city council. He had to find out if Brian and Lydia were right about the city council's goals before he could start putting his ideas together. Miss Claudia called him back in a few minutes. The other council members had agreed to meet at four o'clock. After that he hoped he'd know what direction to take.

Dani wasn't sure how she managed to accomplish anything the rest of the day. Her mind was so busy thinking about what she'd wear that evening, wondering if she should go get her hair trimmed after work, and telling herself to calm down. Thad might want her company for dinner, but that didn't mean he wanted a relationship with her.

Still, she felt like a teenager about to go on her first date. She was nervous and excited and could think of little else. As she watched the weather report, though, she told herself she'd better enjoy the evening because she might be thinking about something entirely different in the next several days. It appeared the storm was now officially named Hurricane Nell and was chugging along at quite a clip. Nell could be in the gulf in a matter of days.

Dani had just finished sending up a prayer for any and all who might be in its path when Claudia knocked on the open door.

"Miss Claudia, come in! What brings you here today? I thought the council meeting was scheduled for next Monday."

"It was. But Thad asked to meet with us, so we're having a special meeting in a few minutes. Do you think you can come on such short notice?"

Dani looked at her schedule and nodded. "I can. Do you know what he wanted to discuss?"

Claudia shook her head. "No. But I'm sure it has something to do with the ad campaign."

"Well, let's go see what he has to say," Dani said. She wondered why he hadn't told her he wanted to meet with the council, but perhaps something had come up since she'd seen him at breakfast.

Thad was waiting with several other members of the council when she and Claudia walked into the room. He seemed at ease and happy to see the two of them so she had to believe that whatever it was he needed to discuss, it had come up since she'd last seen him.

The meeting was called to order, and they got down to business with Claudia formally addressing Thad.

"What is it you wanted to talk to us about, Mr. Cameron?"

"Well, as I've already explained to you, Miss Claudia, I've never tried to sell a town before, and I've been having a problem coming up with the right hook. I think it may be that I don't understand how you want to bring Magnolia Bay back to prosperity. I talked to several people in town today and found out the council may be trying to bring more than tourists in to Magnolia Bay—that maybe you'd like to draw in more industry."

Claudia looked as confused as Dani felt. Formality went out the window. "I'm not sure what you're talking about, Thad. While I like the idea, this is the first I've heard of it." Claudia looked around the table. "Can any of you shed some light on what Thad has heard?"

Morris Gentry sighed and stood up. "We were going to bring it up at the next regular meeting, but now is as good a time as any. Ed and I and several other members of the Downtown Association have been a little worried about counting on only tourists to help us grow again. At present we don't even have enough restaurants or motels to accommodate many tourists."

"That's true enough," Fredrick Denison said. "But what have you come up with?"

"Several internet and computer-geared companies in the area might be interested in bringing their businesses here to Magnolia Bay, if we make it worth their while," Ed Jenson said.

"What do you mean 'worth their while,' Ed? We can't afford to pay businesses to come in here," Tim Hays said.

"No, but we could give them a tax break for the first few years," Ed replied. "And we have several empty buildings out by the highway that we could rent out inexpensively. The thing we do seem to have plenty of is housing."

"I like the idea, but why haven't you brought it up before now?" Claudia asked.

"It's only just come up. My son-in-law works for one of the companies, and they contacted me because of him," Morris said. "I did tell several members of the Downtown Association that we might discuss bringing in some industry at our next meeting. It makes sense to me. Even if we give the businesses a tax break, if we can get more people to move in, then we'll gain by the taxes they will pay as residents here—sales tax, property tax, gasoline tax."

"I sure like that idea better than only trying to draw more tourists," Claudia admitted. "Not that we don't need them, too. But I don't want us to turn into another spring break destination any more than I want us to have casinos here—not unless we can draw a spring break crowd that just wants a nice peaceful place to enjoy the sun and surf."

"If done right, you could probably target a group like that who had no interest in, or wouldn't be allowed to go to, some of the wilder spring break destinations," Thad said. "But I think you're on the right track by trying to draw industry to the area. I just needed to make sure that what I'd heard was right."

"Are you still willing to work with us?" Morris asked.

Dani listened closely to Thad's reply.

He nodded. "Oh, yes, more now than before. I think you've answered all the questions I needed you to address. When we first talked I was under the impression you were interested only in tourists. Trying to draw more industry, however, so that people will have work and others will move in, plus targeting a different kind of tourist, makes a lot more sense to me. I didn't want to see this town lose its charm. Now I think I can come up with something that will help keep Magnolia Bay the way we want it to stay and help you bring in more people too."

For the first time since the advertising campaign had been decided on, Dani felt good about it. Thad was obviously sincere in wanting the best for her town. She said a silent prayer that the Lord would help him do just that.

eleven

When the meeting adjourned, several of the council members gathered around Thad, asking him questions, giving him their opinions, and telling him to take whatever time he needed to come up with a plan. Dani would like to have been in on it all; but knowing she was going to see Thad later that night and could ask him to fill her in, she hurried back to her office to finish up for the day.

She wanted to look her best that evening, and she hadn't bought anything new to wear in a long time, so she stopped by Meagan's Color Cottage on the way home. Meagan had left for the day, but her assistant manager, Sara, helped Dani find an outfit she loved.

After trying on several different ones and turning this way and that in front of a three-way mirror, she finally decided on an amethyst sundress that came with a striped jacket of the same shade of purple and turquoise.

"Oh, that is it," Sara said. "It makes the color of your eyes appear even deeper. It looks wonderful on you, Dani."

She thought it brought out the color of her eyes, too, and was glad Sara agreed. "Thanks. I like it too. I'll take it."

She found earrings and a necklace to match and felt good about her purchases as she left the store. But it had taken much longer than she'd planned. By the time she arrived home she barely had time to shower, apply fresh makeup, and change into her new dress.

It was worth it, though, when she opened the door and saw Thad's reaction. His gaze drifted from the top of her head to the turquoise shoes she had on, before coming back to rest on her face. "You look lovely, Dani. That dress is almost an exact match for your eyes tonight."

"Is it?" That was the reason she'd bought it, but she hadn't expected him to notice.

He looked at her intently. "Oh, yes, it is. At least for tonight—tomorrow they will be a different shade."

"They will?"

"Mmm." His gaze moved to her lips. "They seem to be a different shade every time I see you."

He'd evidently given the color of her eyes more than a little thought. Dani's heart beat faster at his comment, and suddenly she couldn't find her voice. All she could manage was a small smile.

❧

Thad cleared his throat, and his gaze met hers once more. "Ah, well, I—are you ready to go?" He changed the subject, as if embarrassed at his admission.

"I am," Dani managed to answer, feeling a warm flush creep up her neck. "Let me just grab my jacket."

Thad helped her on with it and waited while she gathered up her purse. She locked the door, and they started up the walk toward his car, his hand at her back.

Somehow tonight felt different from any other time they'd been together. This felt like a real date, and just the thought of that had Dani's pulse racing double time as Thad opened the car door for her. Not wanting him to see how nervous she was, Dani took a deep breath and tried to compose herself before he got into the driver's seat. She hoped he couldn't tell how his words had affected her.

Searching for anything to say, she decided it would be best to get things back on a business footing. "Did the meeting today help you?"

He started the car and put it in gear. "Oh, yes. I have several ideas fighting to be put down on paper. I can't wait to get started."

"You could have cancelled our dinner tonight if you needed to work, Thad." But she was glad he hadn't.

"Oh, I'm not in that big of a hurry." He grinned at her before backing out and heading toward Bay Drive. "It can wait until tomorrow."

"I'm glad you asked for the meeting. I feel so much better knowing the council wants to revive Magnolia Bay in the right way. I was worried about that."

"I know. I could tell you weren't happy about the original plan."

"No, I wasn't. I tried not to show it, but it wasn't easy. I'm afraid I wasn't as helpful as I should have been when we first started out."

"You've been wonderful, Dani. I wouldn't have wanted anyone else to show me around Magnolia Bay. Your love of this town came through loud and clear from the beginning, and I respected that you were doing your job even though you obviously didn't agree with what the council seemed to want to do."

"I didn't agree with them. They didn't ask my opinion, though, and I didn't give it. Maybe I should have. But the

Lord answers prayers in all kinds of ways, and I think this newest development is definitely an answer to prayer."

"I think you may be right," Thad said as he pulled into the parking lot of the Seaside Surf and Turf.

❧

Thad couldn't put his finger on it, but things felt different tonight. It was as if there'd been a subtle change in his and Dani's relationship. . .if it could be called that. She seemed more. . .he didn't know. Maybe the change was within him.

When she'd opened the door, looking absolutely beautiful, Thad knew without a doubt he was falling in love with her. His fear of being hurt had taken a backseat to testing the waters during the past few days, and he no longer had control over whether he was hurt again. He wanted to be with her more than he wanted to protect his heart. Thad sent up a prayer that she would come to care for him too—if not now, then eventually.

As they were shown a table and given menus, Thad was just happy she was with him.

"It all sounds good tonight," Dani said, as she looked over the menu. "It's always hard for me to decide what I want, but I think I'll go with the shrimp fettuccini."

"That sounds good, but I think I'll go with—"

The waiter came to the table just then.

"The lady will have the shrimp fettuccini, and I'll try the surf platter," he said before the waiter could ask for their orders. When he left the table, Thad looked over to see Dani shaking her head. "What did I do?"

She chuckled and grinned. "Lori would never believe

you are hungry enough for the seafood platter after the breakfast you ate this morning."

The fact that she seemed comfortable enough to tease him gave him hope that maybe tonight *was* different for her too. She seemed more. . .open. . .more. . .trusting? He didn't know what it was, but something seemed to have changed, and he hoped it wasn't only wishful thinking on his part.

"You helped me with that."

"Oh, right. I really did, didn't I?" She laughed.

He gave an exaggerated sigh. "I guess I'll have to jog when I get back to the inn tonight."

Dani chuckled then turned serious. "Better enjoy it if you go for one. This nice weather we've been having may be about to change."

Thad nodded. "Cole told me the storm is called Hurricane Nell now."

"Yes, and so far she's not showing any sign of changing course."

Her brow furrowed as she seemed lost in thought. Thad could tell she was concerned. "How far out would you start gearing up as a town?"

"Well, watches are usually issued at about seventy-two hours out, and we receive updates every six hours from the hurricane center. Then we have a lot of conference calls with national, state, and local authorities. Once a warning is issued, usually at twenty-four hours out, then—depending on the speed of movement, it might be issued earlier—we get updates every three hours."

"And you stay where?"

"I'll be at city hall along with the department heads of our city and emergency services."

"But that's only a few blocks from the bay, Dani."

"The building has been there a long time, Thad," Dani tried to assure him. "But the storm is not even in the gulf yet. Maybe it won't get here."

"I hope not."

"You might want to think of going back to Dallas if a warning is issued."

No. Thad didn't want to think about that. The waiter brought their dinners then, and they managed to keep the weather out of the conversation throughout the rest of the evening. But Thad was pretty sure it was at the back of both their minds. He was full when they left the restaurant. Since it was a beautiful evening out he suggested a stroll along the bay's boardwalk, hoping she would take pity on him for eating too much. He wasn't ready for the evening to end.

"Please walk with me, Dani. I won't be able to jog at all if I don't walk some of this off now."

She laughed but agreed. "All right. But I don't think you'll be able to jog even with a walk first."

"Probably not, but a walk is better than nothing."

"That's true," Dani said as they headed away from the restaurant.

They strolled more than walked, observed the moon and the stars, debated on whether it was a ship's lights they saw offshore or not, and talked about anything else that came to mind. With the moonlight shining across the bay and Dani beside him, walking with her was much better than jogging with Cole. Much better.

The breeze picked up off the bay. "I guess we'd better turn back," Dani said. "I probably need to check on the weather."

Much as Thad wanted to keep the evening going, he immediately turned toward the restaurant. With that storm out there, she had responsibilities that were probably weighing heavily on her.

"When were you planning to return to Dallas?" she asked as they walked back to his car.

"I'd planned on being here several more weeks."

"Well, if Nell gets much stronger, you might think about leaving earlier."

"Why?"

"Thad, if it gets too bad we'll call for an evacuation."

"But you don't know yet how serious it might be."

"No, not at the moment. But—"

"Well, why don't we take a wait-and-see attitude about it for now?" Thad opened the passenger door for Dani, and she slid inside.

She looked up at him and smiled. "I guess we can do that."

Thad's question had been in connection with the storm, but looking down into those beautiful eyes of hers, he suddenly wasn't sure if he was referring to the storm or their relationship. All he knew was he wanted to kiss her.

"Thad?" Dani broke into his thoughts.

"Yes?"

"Are you all right?"

No. He was in love. "Sorry. I was just lost in my thoughts." He walked around and slid into the car. That wasn't totally true. He was lost in his dreams.

❧

Dani hated for the evening to come to an end. As Thad pulled up outside her home and came around to open her door, she felt like Cinderella must have when the clock struck midnight. At least Dani's prince was seeing her to the door, but that only delayed the inevitable.

"I really enjoyed the evening, Dani. Thank you for going with me," Thad said as she unlocked her door.

"Thank you for asking me. I enjoyed it, too." She didn't know what to say next, and the silence that ensued wasn't as comfortable as usual.

"I hope we can do it again."

"That would be nice."

Thad nodded. "Good. I know you'll be very busy the next few days if that storm does pose a threat, but I'll be praying it doesn't." He hesitated a moment before placing his hands on her shoulders and lowering his head.

Dani's heart seemed to stop beating as Thad's lips lightly touched hers for a moment. . .and then two. . .and then. . . she found herself responding as he deepened the kiss.

She didn't know for sure who finally broke it off, but suddenly they stood there gazing into each other's eyes.

"They are," Thad stated.

"Are what?" Dani couldn't seem to pull her gaze away from his.

"Your lips are as soft as I thought they might be."

"Ooh. . . ."

"Thank you again for tonight. I'll be praying old Nell doesn't keep you awake."

"Thank you." But Dani didn't think Nell would keep her

awake. More than likely it would be thoughts of the kiss they'd just shared.

Thad backed off her front porch and left her with a wave of his hand, and Dani waited until he got into the car before going inside. She let out a huge sigh. What was she thinking responding to that kiss the way she had? No way could he not know she cared about him now. And no way could she continue to hide her growing feelings for him.

She'd been weaving a dream all evening, but that's all it was—a dream. Thad was doing his best to help Magnolia Bay; but his home was still in Dallas, and hers was not. Her life was here in this town with these people. She didn't want a long-distance romance and couldn't see herself relocating.

Besides, one kiss didn't mean he was in love with her. He'd wanted to find out if her lips were soft. He had an answer, and for her heart's sake, she didn't need to start reading anything more into it.

Frustrated with herself, Dani flipped on the television and found the weather channel. Nell had entered the Gulf of Mexico, but early forecasts had it heading for Texas. Still, some of the models had it turning. She could only leave things in the Lord's hands and go to bed. Things would be clearer in the morning. . .at least weather-wise.

Her relationship with Thad seemed to be getting muddier all the time.

twelve

The next morning brought no good news. Nell seemed to be stalled in the gulf, and that could signal more than one thing. The storm could strengthen, or it could be getting ready to make a turn. No one knew what it was going to do, but one thing seemed certain. It showed no sign of weakening.

Thad was right. She was going to be pretty busy the next few days. As Dani got ready for work, she thought it was good she would be busy. . .as far as her relationship with Thad was concerned. She needed some space from him. She'd slept fitfully most of the night, and the first thought on her mind this morning hadn't been Nell. It had been Thad and their kiss, just as she'd known it would be. She would be thinking about that kiss for many days to come, but right now she had to put it in the back of her mind and concentrate on the storm in the gulf.

Magnolia Bay could be Nell's target, and if that was the case Dani had to have a clear mind while she dealt with it. She had to quit thinking about Thad Cameron.

As soon as she arrived at work, she called for a meeting with her emergency management team. Everyone reported that their departments were as ready as they were going to be in the planning state. The test would be when, and if,

Nell headed toward Magnolia Bay.

Chief of police Harvey Baker said his people were ready to start going from house to house if warnings were issued and an evacuation was ordered. Some of the older residents who'd made it through many a storm could be downright stubborn at times. But the police department would be out in force trying to get them to go.

The fire and rescue team was prepared to transport patients from the nursing home should they need to get them to higher ground. Once they knew what Nell's track was, if need be, they'd be moved to a hospital that was deemed safe.

"But your people will get off the streets before it comes ashore, right?" Dani wanted reassurance she wouldn't be putting anyone in harm's way.

"Yes, ma'am, they will. We'll be out there as long as it's safe to be; after that anyone who stays will have to wait until the storm has passed if they need help. You can be assured we'll try to get as many of our citizens as we can to safe ground, battened down or out of here, whatever the circumstances require. But I won't send my people out during landfall."

Dani breathed only slightly easier. Now that Nell was in the Gulf of Mexico, there would be no relaxing until after she came ashore and began to weaken. Even if she hit somewhere else, the tension would be there up until the end. Some hurricanes had been known to bounce all around the gulf before coming ashore. Dani prayed that Nell wasn't that kind of storm.

❧

Thad watched the morning news with Cole, Ronni, and

Claudia. He could feel the tension climb in the room.

"I don't like the looks of this one," Cole said, watching the television screen intently.

"No, neither do I," Miss Claudia said, taking a sip of coffee.

Ronni sighed and shook her head.

"I admit to knowing hardly anything about hurricanes, and I know the worry is that it could come here, but what makes you all so worried about this one in particular, compared to—say, the last storm that went into the gulf?"

"Well, they're all cause for concern because they can change so quickly. But this one already has a tight eye wall." Cole walked over to the television and pointed to the center of the storm. "It seems to be strengthening. Some storms never become that well defined. We'll know more after the hurricane hunters from Biloxi go out later today."

"They fly into it?"

"Yes, they do. They fly right into the eye. The National Hurricane Center gathers a wealth of information from them."

Thad stared at the television screen. "I'm not sure I'd want that job."

"Oh, I know I wouldn't. But I'm glad someone does."

"I imagine Dani is gearing up for the possibility that it might come this way," Ronni said.

"Oh, yes, she is," Miss Claudia said. "She's going to update the council members this afternoon. We should all know more by then."

Thad hoped so. He should have paid more attention to things through the years—and been praying for those who lived on the coast, especially at this time of year.

"Mom, I guess we'd better go down and answer some of our guests' questions," Ronni said, taking a last sip from her coffee cup.

"Yes. Some of them may decide to cut their visits short, and I can't say I blame them," Miss Claudia said, standing and looking at Cole and Thad. "Are you two coming down for breakfast?"

"You go on," Cole said. "We'll be down as soon as we finish this coffee."

"We'll see you in a few minutes," Ronni said, giving her husband a kiss before going down on the elevator with Miss Claudia.

Thad needed no reminder of the kiss he'd shared with Dani. He'd been trying to put it out of his mind ever since he woke up this morning. He was sure she'd responded to his kiss. He could almost feel the touch of her lips on his. But now wasn't the time to be dwelling on it. . .at least not until Dani had less on her mind than a hurricane that could be heading this way.

"Are you going to stay with us or head back to Dallas, my friend?" Cole asked as they finished their coffee

Thad wasn't about to leave yet. "I'm staying for now— unless you need the room?"

"No." Cole shook his head. "I just wanted you to know we'd understand if you decide to go back to Dallas for a few days."

"What I'd like to do is look at a few homes on the market around here."

"Really?"

"Yes. I think I may do as you did and move here."

Cole's enthusiasm was clear. "Oh, wow, Thad! That would be so great." He smiled. "Dani Phillips wouldn't have anything to do with your decision, would she?"

"She might. She doesn't know it yet, though."

"Oh, I see."

"And I don't know how she will feel about it, but I've pretty much decided it's what I want to do. Now just isn't the time to let her know."

"I understand. I had the same problem with Ronni. I pray it all works out for you, Thad. I think you and Dani would make a wonderful couple."

"So do I. I guess time will tell. Meanwhile I'll need a place to live until I can convince her we would."

"Several wonderful homes are for sale in the older part of Magnolia Bay, and you know I'd be glad to draw up plans for you, if new is what you would want."

"I'm counting on it."

"Well, let's get going. We can check into some listings after breakfast. We have a friend who is a realtor, and I'm sure he'd be glad to show you around. I'd like to tag along if it's all right with you."

"Sure, it's all right with me. If I find something that would need work, you'd be able to tell me what that might entail. I just figured you'd be busy—"

"Oh, I've got things I could do, but nothing pressing

right now. And, believe me—with this storm churning up out there I'd be better off going with you instead of watching the weather channel all day."

"Let's do it then." Thad pulled a paper out of his wallet and handed it to Cole. "Please give him this list of homes I'd like to look at and see if he can line them up for us."

"Sounds like a plan." Cole called Joe Morgan, a longtime friend and well-known realtor in the area, and told him the homes Thad wanted to see. He gave Thad the thumbs-up sign as he finished the conversation. "That sounds great, Joe. We'll meet you at your office in about forty-five minutes."

He hung up the receiver and stood. "Come on. Let's grab some breakfast, and we'll meet Joe. He said he'd line up as many homes on your list as he could. I think he's glad of the chance to get away from the television, too."

As they headed downtown after a breakfast of scrambled eggs, bacon, and croissants, Thad was relieved he had something concrete to do. He wanted to talk to Dani, wanted to see how she was doing today. Wanted to tell her he loved her, wanted to kiss her again.

But he was certain she had more on her mind today than their kiss last night, and he would need to be patient. The time was coming when he'd be able to tell her how he felt—but it wasn't today.

"What made you decide you want to move here, Thad?" Joe Morgan asked as they started up the walk of a stately home on Bay Drive.

"Well, Cole told me that if I hung around Magnolia

Bay long enough I'd end up wanting to live here. I guess he was right." He knew he wasn't telling him everything. Dani had a lot to do with his decision—but not all. He prayed it would work out the way he wanted it to between the two of them, but he'd been thinking of making the move even before he fell in love with her. If it didn't work out it wouldn't be easy, but he knew the Lord would get him through the pain. He'd done it before, and Thad knew he could count on Him again.

"Well, you might change your mind if Nell decides to visit our town."

"Might. But I doubt it. Are either of you planning to move away?"

Joe laughed. "Not likely. My family has been here for generations. Our roots go deep."

"Not me. It took me too long to make the move as it is. I'm not about to leave now."

"Enough said?" Thad grinned at the two men.

"Well, let's see if we can find Thad a home, Cole," Joe said as he unlocked the front door.

By the time they took a lunch break at Beach Burgers, Thad had seen more than one home he knew he could be happy living in. The tough part would be deciding which one to put an offer on or whether to have Cole draw up plans for a new one. In the back of his mind, though, he never quit thinking of Dani; he knew his house decision would hinge on her and whether their relationship had a chance of becoming permanent. If not, he needed to have a plan in mind, and he was glad he'd found so many places from which to choose.

They looked at a few more homes after lunch, and Thad was pleased with the selections. He knew it wouldn't always be this way. Once word got out about Magnolia Bay, and if the town was able to attract industry as it hoped to do, the housing market would tighten up. It was inevitable. But for now he felt no pressure to make a decision.

"Things haven't been moving very fast." Joe confirmed his thought at the end of the day. "If you want to see these homes again or others you might run across, just give me a call."

Thad shook his hand. "I'll be in touch. Thanks for showing me all of these today."

"Thanks for keeping me busy," Joe said. "I love it here, but this watching and waiting can sure get on one's nerves."

"Boy, isn't that the truth," Cole agreed. "Guess it's time to get an update, though."

They parted ways, and Thad and Cole headed back to the inn. He would like to stop by city hall, but the meeting with the city council had probably started by now, and Thad didn't want to get in the way.

They tuned in the television but knew little more than they'd known that morning. Nell was still chugging north but had taken a slight jog to the west.

"That could be good news or not. It could be just a bobble," Cole said. "But, if not, it might mean it's going into Texas. It's hard to know at this stage."

Miss Claudia returned just before dinner to let them know Dani had everything under control.

"For the first time, though, I almost wish we'd hired someone else for the job," she said.

"Why, Aunt Claudia?" Cole asked. "Are you afraid she's not up to the task?"

"Oh, no, dear. I'm confident Dani is very capable. But I've come to care for her so much, as if she's part of the family, and I hate for her to be under such a strain."

So did Thad. And there was no way for him to ease it for her. He hoped this storm decided what it was going to do soon; while Dani was uppermost in his mind he was pretty sure he was way down the list in hers.

❧

Dani was exhausted by the time she left the office that night. Hurricane Nell had taken a jog to the west, but the computer models seemed to be split on which direction she was heading. Some said she would go into Texas and another into Louisiana, but a couple of them predicted a Mississippi landfall. For the moment it looked as if it would be the Texas coast, but Dani knew Magnolia Bay wasn't out of danger yet.

She picked up an order to go from Beach Burgers and drove home. She didn't want to think about Nell until morning. There was nothing more to be done until then. The city services were ready and on standby. She was going to eat her burger, take a shower, and pack a bag to take to work the next morning—in case she had to stay at city hall.

Mostly she was going to try *not* to think about Thad Cameron, but she already knew that wouldn't be easy to do. He'd been in the back of her mind all day. From the time she awakened that morning, clear through to the meeting with the city council—thoughts of Thad had warred with Hurricane Nell for her attention.

But he hadn't called or come by her office, and she told herself she was silly for spending any time at all thinking about him. Clearly that kiss hadn't meant as much to him as it had to her.

Dani ate her supper, took a shower, and packed her bag. Then she sat down to watch the latest weather update. No change—it had barely moved. She took a deep breath and sent a prayer heavenward.

"Dear Lord, please let this storm burn itself out in the gulf. If it does come ashore anywhere, please let its damage be minimal and protect all of those in its path. Should it come this way, please give me the wisdom and strength to do what is needed for this town." Dani paused for a moment before adding, "And, dear Lord, please help me to get Thad out of my thoughts and heart. In Jesus' precious name I pray, amen."

Dani locked up and made sure her cordless telephone was in its holder close to her bed, in case she was called during the night. Only then did she notice the blinking light signaling she had a message. She punched play and waited.

"Dani, it's me, Thad. It's seven o'clock, and I wanted to check in with you and see how your day went. I know you have a lot on your mind with Nell out there, but if you aren't too tired when you get home please give me a call." He gave her his cell phone number, and then she heard a pause before he finished with, "I missed you at breakfast today. Talk to you later."

Dani placed her hand over her heart and sighed. Here she'd thought he didn't care, that he hadn't tried to contact her. She looked at the clock. It was eleven-thirty and too late to call tonight. Tears welled up and fell over her lashes, and Dani began to cry. Now Thad must think *she* was awful for not returning *his* call.

thirteen

Thad tossed and turned all night. Dani hadn't returned his call. He didn't know if she hadn't called because it was too late when she got home or because she didn't want to talk to him. He meant to find out, though, as soon as he could.

It was too early to get up and about. He didn't want to wake Miss Claudia or the Bannisters, but he had to find out what Nell was doing out in the gulf. He turned on the small television in his room with the volume low and flipped channels until he found the weather channel. What he saw and heard took the breath out of him.

Nell had strengthened during the night and was a strong category two. The hurricane center was expecting her to be a category three by that evening. But worse than that, she'd taken a northeastern turn, and now the forecasts had her coming in somewhere along the Mississippi coast. It looked as if she'd be coming right over Magnolia Bay. The hurricane watch the town had been in was now a warning, and Thad felt sick at the thought of what it could do to this town.

He bent his head and prayed with everything in him that the Lord would keep this town and the people in it safe. . . and especially that He would keep Dani safe. He looked at the alarm clock on the bedside table. Six thirty. If Cole and Ronni weren't up by now they soon would be, and he was pretty sure Miss Claudia would have the coffeepot on while she watched the same report.

Thad threw back his covers and went to shower. He wanted to go to city hall and check on Dani as soon as he could. After taking a quick shower he dressed, made up his bed, and went out to find he was right. Miss Claudia had put on the coffeepot and was looking at the television.

"Oh, Thad, dear. Have you seen?" The worry was evident in her eyes when she turned to him.

"Yes, ma'am, I have."

"I've told Dani and the city council that Bay Inn can serve as a shelter for those who can't stay in their homes but won't leave town. What are you going to do? Are you heading back to Dallas, or will you see it out with us?"

"No, Miss Claudia, I'm not leaving. I'm staying here unless you need my room. I can't leave when Dani—." Thad broke off, but not before Miss Claudia smiled.

"Ahh. It's like that, is it?"

Thad shrugged and grinned. "It's like that on my part. I'm not sure about Dani. But I'm not about to leave while she's under so much pressure."

"You're a good man, Thad Cameron. I hope she realizes it."

"Thank you, Miss Claudia. So do I."

Cole and Ronni joined them in the kitchen. The look on their faces told Thad they'd been watching the news from their room.

Ronni poured herself a cup of coffee and blew on it before taking a drink.

"I guess we'd better go make it easy for our guests to check out. After talking to them yesterday, I don't think many will want to stay," Miss Claudia said.

"No, I don't think they will either."

"I'll start boarding up the windows on the ground floor," Cole said. "After I finish ours I'll go downtown and see who needs help."

"I'm going to check on Dani," Thad said. Cole and Miss Claudia already knew or suspected how he felt about her. It was a pretty good guess that Ronni did, too. "I'll come back to help you board up after I talk to her."

"Thanks, Thad."

Thad downed his coffee and took off. If Dani wasn't already at city hall, she was sure to be soon. When he spotted her car in the parking lot, he let out a sigh. He hoped she'd been able to go home and get some sleep last night.

It looked chaotic outside the building, where they were boarding up windows, and inside, where people seemed to be going in all directions. But Thad supposed that was normal under the circumstances. He found Dani in her office on the telephone. She motioned him in, and he waited while she finished her conversation. She looked tired. . .and stressed. He wished he could do something to make this easier for her.

She finished her call and hung up the receiver. "I'm sorry I didn't return your call last night, Thad. I didn't see the message until after it was too late to call you back."

"It's all right, Dani. I just wanted to check on you. I was pretty sure you had a hectic day."

"You could say that. But I'm all right. I guess you know we're now under a hurricane warning?"

Thad nodded. "I saw in the news. Looks as if you'll be busy for the next few days."

"Yes, it does."

"It's hectic out there." Thad pointed to the hall outside her office.

"It is. They're setting up the bunker."

"The bunker?"

"Come on. I'll show you," Dani said, leading the way out of her office.

She led him to a windowless room in the center of the building. As Thad watched, he realized these people knew what they were doing.

"It's called the 'bunker' because it's the safest room in city hall," Dani said. "All the city services set up command centers here when we're under a hurricane warning. It's been somewhat reinforced and is supposed to withstand category three or more hurricane winds. But we're hoping we never get one big enough to test that theory."

Thad hoped not too. He felt better knowing she wouldn't be in her office with all the windows, but not much. "Is there anything I can do to help you?"

Dani shook her head. "We're calling for an evacuation, Thad. You need to get in your car and drive back to Texas."

Thad shook his head. No way would he leave her behind. "I can't do that. I'm not leaving town, Dani."

"Thad, you asked what you could do to help me. I don't need to be worrying about you. You don't know what a storm like this can do. You've never been through a hurricane, and now isn't the time to see what it would be like. Nell isn't a nice lady. You need to evacuate."

Thad knew he'd never been truly in love until now. All he wanted was to make sure this woman was all right, and he would not leave town while she was in jeopardy. "I know I've never been through a hurricane before. And I don't want to get in your way. But I'm not going back to Texas, so tell me what I can do to help."

She let out a big sigh, and he could tell she was exasperated with him, but he seemed to have convinced her he wasn't going anywhere. "See if anyone needs help boarding up their homes or businesses. And then go back up to Bay Inn and stay there until this is over. Please."

"Miss Phillips—we need you over here a minute," the chief of police called.

"I'll be right there." Dani looked up at Thad. "I have to go. Please leave, Thad. Go back to Texas. That's really what you could do for me."

Before he could say anything else, she was on her way across the room. She had a job to do, and he needed to let her do it. He wanted to make things easier for her—but he wasn't about to leave town.

❧

Dani looked over her shoulder to see Thad walk away, and suddenly she felt like crying. But she couldn't give in to the urge to run back to her office and bawl like a baby. She had a job to do, and she had to see it through. *Don't cry. . .don't cry. . .don't cry—*

"You all right, Dani?" the chief asked.

"I'm fine, chief. Or will be once we see this storm through." Finally feeling as if she could keep her tears at bay, she looked up at the older man. "What did you need?"

"We wanted to know how you want to handle those citizens who refuse to leave their homes."

"We can't take them by force. What do you suggest?"

"Well, several other departments along the coast have told their people that if they aren't leaving they need to write their Social Security numbers and the phone numbers of their next of kin on their arms, so officials know whom to notify if they don't make it through. I thought we could give that a try. Maybe it will wake up a few of them so they realize they need to get out."

Dani let out her breath with a whoosh as they walked back to her office. "That's pretty vivid, but it might work. I say let's go for it."

"It won't hurt to try. Some of those old-timers are just plain stubborn, and I don't understand why. I can still remember Camille, and I hope we don't have to go through that again."

"Oh, chief, I hope we can get the people living down near the coast to leave. I pray we're ready for whatever happens."

"You've done a fine job of leading us and getting us ready for this, Dani. I've been through a lot of storms on the coast, but I've never felt we were as ready as we are now. We started our emergency preparedness meetings a full month earlier than usual. I know there was a lot of grumbling about it at the time, but we all feel much more prepared than we have in the past—before the city hired you. Your dad would be very proud."

"Thank you, Chief. I needed to hear that." Chief Baker's words meant more to Dani than she could say, and she fought to hold back the tears that gathered at the back of her eyes.

Harvey Baker was about her dad's age, and they'd been good friends. The chief had watched her grow up. Ever since Dani had been hired as city manager he'd watched over her carefully, and she'd felt she must live up to his and her dad's expectations. Tonight his words made her feel as if he thought she had.

She swallowed around the lump in her throat and forced herself to speak. "We're supposed to get another update in about an hour. After that I think we'll have to start sending out your patrolmen to tell people to leave."

"I agree. I'll go spread the word to be on the ready."

"Thanks, Chief."

When she sat down at her desk, Dani realized how tired she was. She'd barely slept the night before, and it didn't look as if she'd be going home tonight. She closed her eyes and rubbed the back of her neck. The Lord would get her through the next few days—she knew He would.

She stood and poured herself a cup of coffee from the pot on a table in the corner of the room. Only when she sat back down did she realize a folded piece of paper with her name on it was lying in the middle of her desk. She opened it.

Dani, I'll try not to get in the way, but I'm staying in Magnolia Bay. If you need me for anything please call my cell or the inn. Thad

What she *needed* was to know he was safe. She needed him to go back to Texas or anywhere else where he wouldn't be in danger. But it appeared the old-timers weren't the only stubborn people in this town. She bowed her head and prayed for the Lord to keep Thad safe.

fourteen

Thad left city hall exasperated. He could do nothing to help Dani except pray, and he'd be doing that from now until this crisis was over. Other than that he figured the best thing was to stay busy.

He called Cole's cell phone to see where he was and if he needed help at the inn.

"Thanks, Thad. I'm nearly finished here. Several of our guests who are staying pitched in and helped. After we get through here I'll be heading downtown to see who I can help."

"I'll find out what I can do from here then," Thad said.

"Okay. I'm sure I'll run into you later."

Thad walked down to Bay Drive and headed toward the Waters Flower Shop and Meagan's Color Cottage to see if he could help them out. Brad was more than happy to have his help nailing up plywood that had been cut to fit each window. Once they were finished, he joined Thad to find out if they could assist other businesses that were across from the bay.

Thad was glad Beach Burgers had been boarded up and secured as well as it could be. But if Nell came ashore in the vicinity he wasn't sure anything would protect the small building.

"Whew," Brad said. "I'm sure glad my business is a little farther away than that one."

"Yeah, I know what you mean. I'm not sure it will be here once this is all over." He sent up a silent prayer that the eatery would be spared.

They found Nick outside Meagan's shop. The upstairs windows were covered, but he was just beginning to board up the windows on the first floor.

"Hey, Nick. You need some help?" Thad called when they were near enough for him to hear.

"Boy, am I glad to see you guys!" Nick accepted the men's offer with enthusiasm. "I sure could use some help. I spent the last few hours boarding up the windows at our house and the upstairs windows of the shop. After I get these finished, I still have to do my office."

"Let's get at it then. Cole said he'd be downtown soon. He was just finishing up Bay Inn when I called him from city hall."

"How's Dani doing?" Nick asked.

"Probably a lot better than I would be if I were in her place. I sure wish I could talk her into moving their command center farther inland."

"Well, it is several blocks away from the shore, and I know they have the bunker. But if I were you, I'd be feeling the same way. Tori, Grams, Meagan, and I are heading for Meagan's parents' place at Hide-a-Way Lake this afternoon."

"Lydia and I are heading inland, too," Brad said.

"What are you doing, Thad?" Nick asked. "Are you staying at the inn?"

"Yes, unless I can convince Dani to let me stay with her at the office."

Nick shook his head. "She goes by the rules, and they don't allow that, Thad. I wouldn't count on it."

Judging from his and Dani's conversation earlier, Thad thought Nick was probably right. But he wasn't giving up until he'd tried to get her to safer ground or let him stay at city hall with her.

Cole showed up about the time they finished boarding up the shop, and for the rest of the morning and early afternoon the men joined others in town boarding and securing as many businesses and homes as they could.

"What about Dani's house? Do you think we should board it up?" Thad asked.

"It sure wouldn't hurt. Call her and find out if she has any boards we can use or if we need to go to the lumberyard and see if they have any plywood left," Cole suggested.

Glad for any excuse to talk to Dani, Thad punched in her phone number on his cell phone. It rang several times before she answered it.

"Hello?"

"Dani, Nick, Cole, and I along with several others are helping out boarding up. We thought maybe we ought to take care of your house, too. Do you have any plywood cut to fit, or do we need to get some?"

There was silence on the other end of the line for a moment. "I'm probably okay, but, yes, there are some boards in the old carriage house at the back of my property. You really don't have to—"

"We know. We want to." Afraid she'd protest more, Thad said, "I'll check with you later. Bye." He ended the call and looked at the three men. "She says she has boards in the carriage house."

"Let's go then."

By the time they'd boarded up Dani's house it was late afternoon. As they headed back through town it was almost eerie the way downtown Magnolia Bay seemed deserted now that most of the buildings were boarded up. A shiver ran down Thad's spine.

Cole had talked to Ronni and informed him that Miss Claudia and Ronni had been cooking all morning and wanted one of them to take some food to city hall for everyone who was manning the bunker.

Thad was quick to volunteer. "I imagine you want to make sure everything is done at the inn. I'll run the food back in. Maybe I can talk Dani into letting me stay there."

"It won't happen, my friend. But I could be wrong, and I can understand why you want to see her and try to convince her to let you stay."

"Thanks."

"You know—while you're there—you might want to let her know how you feel about her," Cole advised.

Thad could only nod. Cole was right, but he didn't trust his voice to answer him. Thad's heart twisted in his chest as he realized why his friend had made the suggestion. It might be his only chance to let Dani know he loved her.

✿

By six o'clock a mandatory evacuation was ordered for

Magnolia Bay. Nell was coming their way. The day had passed in a blur for Dani as she received updates and participated in conference calls with national and state officials and city officials along the coast who were getting ready for this hurricane.

Nell would more than likely be a category three by the time she came on shore. With winds at 111 to 130 miles per hour, the damage could be widespread. The chief had his men out on the roads trying to convince residents to heed the warnings, but before long they could do nothing except get off the streets, hunker down, and wait it out.

Dani hadn't had much time to think about her friends or how they were faring in preparing for Nell, and she'd purposely tried not to think about Thad. But that had been impossible. When he'd called to ask about her windows she'd been more than a little touched by his thoughtfulness—even though she wished he'd just left town so she wouldn't have to worry about him. But from the time he'd walked out the door of city hall he'd been at the back of her mind ready to sneak into her thoughts any time she had a calm moment.

Now she tried not to think of him as she gathered up papers from her office to take to the bunker when it became necessary. The door opened then, and she didn't know whether to be happy or upset when Thad walked through it, his arms loaded with baskets of delicious-smelling food. She and several others hurried to help him.

"Miss Claudia sent this in for all of you. With everything closed she figured you could use a little home cooking."

"Oh, how sweet of her. We stocked the kitchen, such as it is, but not with anything that smells this good."

"There's more out in my car." Thad had more than enough volunteers to bring it in. Word had gotten around by the time they brought in the pies and cakes Miss Claudia and Ronni had sent, and the small kitchen was crowded with people filling plates.

"You need to eat, too," Thad said to Dani.

"I will." She nodded as she watched her emergency crew line up.

"No, *now*," Thad insisted. "I bet you haven't eaten anything since this morning, and I told Miss Claudia I would make sure you did. I have to keep my word. Do you need me to make a plate for you?"

Dani smiled and shook her head. He was right. She hadn't eaten since breakfast. "No. I'll make it. I'm not hungry, but I know I need to eat."

"Good. I'll keep you company while you do."

"You might as well eat, too, then."

Thad stepped in line behind her. "I think I will. The smells in my car had my mouth watering all the way here."

"I'll have to call Miss Claudia later and thank her. All this food seems to have raised everyone's spirits, at least for a little while."

"She and Ada and Ronni have been cooking most of the day, I think. She said they had a huge freezer, and everything could go bad if the electricity went out for several days. Better to share it than lose it."

"Well, I really appreciate that she did this for us," Dani

said as she led the way back to her office so they could eat at her desk.

Thad said a blessing for the food and was pleased when they started to eat and Dani seemed to have found her appetite. They talked little until they'd both finished.

As Dani gathered up their plates and cups and dropped them in the trash, Thad remembered the message he was supposed to give her. "Oh, yes, Miss Claudia said to remind you the inn is open and ready if anyone needs to take refuge there."

"Thanks. So far we're good. The high school still has some room, and several churches have set up as storm shelters. Unless there is an overflow, I think things will be all right. But please tell her thank you."

"I wish you would go back with me and tell her yourself."

"Thad, you know I can't do that. I'm the city manager of this town. Everyone here is looking to me for guidance, and it's my responsibility to give it."

He sighed. "I know. I do know, Dani—but I hate to leave you here."

Her heart twisted. Dani didn't want him to leave her either. But her job was here, and part of it was to try to keep the people in this town safe. . .including Thad.

"You need to go back to the inn before the weather gets worse. We'll be getting tropical force winds out ahead of the storm soon. Besides, if you don't go back there, Claudia and the Bannisters will be worried about you."

"Let me stay, Dani. I won't get in your way. I promise. I just—"

"You can't stay here, Thad. It's against the rules. The others can't even bring family in here. There's no way I can let you stay." Dani wanted him to stay, but more than that she wanted him to be safe. She stood and walked over to the doorway. "I have enough responsibility right now, Thad. Please don't put more on me."

She could tell Thad was upset as he released a deep breath and shook his head. She steeled herself against his frustration. But when he walked over to her and gently shut the door and pulled her into his arms, her heart almost melted.

"All right, Dani. I'll leave," he promised, looking deep into her eyes. "But I can't leave you here without telling you this. I love you. . .with *all* my heart. And when this is over I'm going to ask you to marry me, so you'd better be prepared to give me an answer."

Dani's breath caught in her throat as Thad lowered his head and kissed her. She could feel his heart beating against hers as she responded. *Thad loved her.*

Her phone started ringing and broke them apart. Dazed, she looked from Thad to the phone.

"I'll go now," Thad said. "I don't want to cause you more stress than you already have. Just know I meant what I said and I'll be praying you stay safe. I love you." With that he gave her a quick kiss on the forehead, turned the knob, and walked out the door.

Dani wanted to call him back. Wanted to tell him she loved him, too—but the phone was still ringing, and she had a job to do. She grabbed the phone on the sixth ring. It was a wrong number. And Thad was gone. Tears streamed down her face as she silently prayed. *Dear Lord, please keep him safe. And if it is Your will, please let me tell him how much I love him when this is all over.*

fifteen

By eleven o'clock Nell had slowed down again, and Dani and the rest of her emergency crew took turns switching channels between WLOX out of Biloxi and the weather channel and monitoring their NOAA weather radio. Nell was a strong category two but was still about forty miles off shore.

It was going to be a long night. A surveillance camera had been set up to look out at the bay. They'd begun to get tropical storm winds from the Louisiana-Mississippi state line clear over to Biloxi, and the chief had his men making their last rounds for the night.

As Nell churned, so did Dani's stomach. She didn't know if it was from watching and waiting for Nell to come ashore or worrying about Thad and how he was dealing with all this, but it wasn't getting any better.

She popped an antacid in her mouth and took a big drink of water, hoping it would give her some relief.

"Want some coffee, Dani?" paramedic Rhonda Lester asked.

Dani shivered and shook her head. "No, thank you. I don't think my stomach would take well to it."

"I understand. I've got the jitters myself. Maybe I'll forgo the coffee, too," Rhonda said.

By midnight the winds had picked up and were whipping

the water in the bay. Chief Baker called his people in off the streets.

The lights flickered, and Dani held her breath as she sent up a prayer that they wouldn't lose power. They could switch to emergency power here, but the rest of the town couldn't. It was bad enough when these storms came through in the daylight. It was much worse when they hit at night.

Nell was getting closer. As they watched the trees bend and sway, the video from the outside monitor shook. The winds were getting stronger. And from looking at the weather channel they were experiencing the same thing to the east. A reporter was trying to stand against the wind and describe what it was like.

The chief shook his head. "I can't believe a reporter is out on the beach with the winds blowing like that," he said. "It never fails to amaze me what a network will do for ratings. No way would I put my people out there like that with a hurricane just offshore."

"I'd hate to think you would! Not to mention that we'd have to fire you if you did." Dani smiled at the chief, but just then a gust of wind hit the building and caught everyone's attention. It wasn't getting any better outside.

☙

Thad paced back and forth, watching the news and listening to the wind gusts as they whirled around, pounding the walls of the inn. Nell was getting closer, and the winds had picked up considerably in the last hour. He couldn't help but wonder how Dani and her crew were holding up. "I wonder how—"

"She's all right, Thad," Cole answered his unfinished question.

But all Thad could bring himself to do in response to Cole's comment was nod. He'd kicked himself over and over for leaving city hall. But Dani hadn't given him much choice, and deep down he knew she didn't need him around to worry about. She had enough to handle.

All he could do was watch the weather reports and pray for her safety—and he'd been doing that ever since he'd left her office. Now, looking at the television screen, he saw that Nell was so close and so large he couldn't figure out exactly where she was or when she was coming ashore. With as little experience as Thad had with hurricanes, he couldn't tell a thing from what he saw.

"She's slowed down again," Cole said. "Maybe she's getting ready to make another turn."

"Or just come barreling on shore," Miss Claudia said.

"What are the chances of her churning herself out?" Thad asked.

"Not very good," Cole answered with a shake of his head. "She could be getting stronger."

The lights flickered, and Thad held his breath. It was hard enough to deal with this storm with the lights and television on. It would be miserable if they lost power.

"Let's set out our candles, Ronni," Miss Claudia said. "We need to have them nearby just in case. I gave some out earlier to the few guests who decided to stay. I hope they're doing okay."

"I'm sure they're glued to the TV just as we are, Aunt

Claudia," Cole said. "But I'll go check on them if you want me to."

She shook her head. "No, that's all right. I called their rooms earlier. They're as safe as we are at present. It's possible they've dozed off, and if so there's no need to waken them now."

As the women set out candles of all sizes, Thad and Cole waited for the next update on the weather channel.

"Look at that guy over in Gulfport," Cole said. "I can't believe these people put their lives in danger to get a news story. After the storm we'll be able to tell how bad it was. *During* it is not time to be out there. I hope they're paying him and his cameraman well."

Thad shook his head as he watched the guy fall down and try to get back up against the wind. "It can't be enough."

The next update gave them no answer to what the storm was doing. There was some speculation that Nell would take an easterly turn and the eye would go over the coast farther down instead of Magnolia Bay, but it was hard to say with the way Nell wobbled back and forth.

"We probably ought to try to get some sleep. A little would be better than none, and we'll have a lot to do once it passes," Cole said. "The best thing we can do now is pray and leave it in the Lord's hands."

Everyone agreed, and before they went to their rooms Cole led them in a prayer.

"Dear Lord, we ask that You watch over this town and all the others along the coast that might be affected by Nell. Please keep us all out of harm's way; please let the damage not be too bad. And please take care of Dani and those with her as they keep watch tonight. This we ask in Jesus' name, amen."

"Amen," Thad added.

He'd showered earlier, and now he turned on the small television in his room, plumped his pillow, and propped himself on it, intending to watch until Nell came on shore. But his mind wandered to Dani, and he relived the moment he'd told her he loved her and kissed her. She'd responded. He knew she had. At least now she knew how he felt. And if something happened—*and, oh, dear Lord, please let that not be the case*—at least she would know he loved her. Somehow that gave him a little comfort as he watched and waited.

He sent up a special prayer for Dani, simply asking the Lord to please keep her safe.

❧

Dani didn't realize she'd dozed off until she heard a cheer go up in the room and her eyes popped open. "What? What is it?"

"Nell is speeding up and changing course! She'll go in just east of us. We'll miss the worst of it," one of her crew shouted.

From the sound of the wind outside they'd been blessed. If it was this strong on the west side of the storm, it was going to be pretty bad on down the coast. Chief Baker handed her a cup of fresh coffee, and Dani thought she might be able to drink it. She didn't know if it was the short nap she'd taken, the news they would be spared a direct hit, or the antacid she'd downed earlier, but her stomach felt better.

As they watched the news, Nell had indeed taken another jog, and they were going to be spared the worst. But Dani could hear the snap of tree limbs outside, and she knew Magnolia Bay wouldn't come out of this unscathed.

"Look at the outside monitor," said Charles Freeman, head of the fire and rescue team. "The water from the bay is being pulled right out and back into the gulf."

"Better that than being thrown up over the town," Harvey said.

Thank You, Lord. Please be with our neighbors to the east. Please keep them out of harm's way and let us be able to help them out if need be.

The lights flickered, and the television went off the air. Obviously their cable signal was gone, but Dani was surprised they hadn't lost it before now.

"We'd better get ready to switch to emergency power. I have a feeling we're going to be in the dark pretty soon," she said.

The words had no more left her mouth than the lights went out, without even a warning flicker. She heard scrambling to start up the emergency system, but in a few minutes the power was back on.

"The weather radio says Nell is coming on shore as a high cat two, maybe a three," the chief said.

The next few hours were the longest Dani could ever remember as they heard what sounded like trees crashing and the wind howling and beating against the building. The bunker might be safe but couldn't drown out the sound of Nell. She didn't want to imagine what the towns were dealing with down the coast.

🍂

Something awakened Thad as the lights went out. It was pitch black in his room. He fumbled to find the lighter and the candle Miss Claudia had placed in there earlier. He'd just lit it when he heard a loud crash outside—then voices coming from the living room. He made his way to the bedroom door.

"Cole? Is that you?"

"Yes, we're out here," Cole answered.

Thad was relieved to see his friend standing in the middle of the living room, lighting one of the candles on the coffee table.

"What was that loud noise?"

"Probably a pine tree landed on something outside. I hope it didn't fall on the house or anyone's car."

"I'll be so glad when this is over," Miss Claudia said, wringing her hands. "I put some coffee in a thermal pot before we tried to get some sleep. It should still be warm. Would any of you like a cup?"

"Yes, please," Cole said, trying to tune in his portable weather radio.

"Me too," Thad said.

"I'll help you," Ronni said, following Miss Claudia into the kitchen. "Can anyone tell what time it is?"

Thad looked at his watch. "It's five fifty."

"Oh, good, it will be light soon. This surely can't last much longer."

Cole zeroed in on the right frequency, and as they listened to the latest update Thad could feel the tension in the room ease. The storm was going in over the stretch of coastline he and Dani had traveled only weeks ago. Bad as the wind sounded from inside the inn, even Thad knew they were not getting the worst of Nell.

"Let's pray," Cole said as the women brought in the coffee cups and took a seat on the sofa. Everyone bowed their heads

"Dear Lord, we thank You that Magnolia Bay has been spared the worst of this storm, but we ask You to be with our neighbors who are in Nell's path. Please be with them and bring them through, and help us be there for them when this is all over. And, Lord, please let this storm be over soon. Amen."

"Amen," Thad echoed. He couldn't wait to go to city hall to make sure Dani was all right.

sixteen

By six thirty Nell was inland and had been reduced to tropical storm status. Dani and the chief decided it was time to see how Magnolia Bay had fared.

She wanted to check on Thad and Claudia and the Bannisters, but both land lines and cell phones were down, leaving them with no telephone service for now. Daylight crews would be out to inspect the damage, though, and start repairing damaged lines and towers as soon as possible.

As Dani, the chief, and the others made their way from the bunker to the outer rooms, she thanked the Lord that Magnolia Bay had escaped the worst of the storm. They went outside and found that city hall was fine, except their outdoor monitor had been torn off the roof along with quite a few shingles. The surrounding buildings seemed to have minimal damage, too. It could have been much worse.

When they looked toward Bay Drive, Dani began praying for those who'd suffered a direct hit by Nell. It had to be bad there. Water in the bay was lower than she'd ever seen it. Although she knew it would soon fill up again, it was shocking. Trees and electrical lines were down here and there on Bay Drive. Some trees were leaning on several homes and businesses, and Dani hoped the damage wasn't as bad as it looked. There also appeared to be roof damage to some of the buildings and homes nearby, but they were still standing tall and proud.

Just the fact that they *were* still there had tears welling up in Dani's eyes. *Thank You, Lord.*

"I'm going to send a couple of patrol cars out to access other parts of town, Dani. There could be flooding in the low-lying areas, and I'm worried about the mobile homes out that way. But let's hope we're seeing the worst of it here."

"A lot of trees are down—do you think it will be safe?"

"My men will come back in if it isn't."

Dani nodded as they went back inside and assigned duties to the team. She tried to concentrate on the work she needed to do, but foremost in her mind, while she tried to determine the extent of the damage her town had suffered, was wondering if Thad was safe. More than anything she wanted to find out how Bay Inn had fared and to make sure Thad and Claudia and the Bannisters were all right.

Crews got their satellite phones up and running. For the next few hours Dani was kept busy receiving updates from down the coast and giving them out as the patrolmen came back in with reports. They'd missed the brunt of the storm but still had damage to contend with. But by midmorning Dani was determined to see the damage for herself.

She took a deep breath and stood up. "Chief, I'd like to

go have a look around town now."

He nodded. "I knew you would. I'll go with you. We'll have to be careful of downed lines too."

"I know. But I need to see how bad it is."

As they started down Bay Drive, Dani's heart broke to see the roof of Beach Burgers torn off. But farther down she was pleased to see Mike's Seaside Surf and Turf seemed to have fared all right. Of course it was newer and had been built to withstand higher winds. Most of the buildings weren't that new, though, and Dani wasn't sure what they'd find.

❧

Thad helped Cole inspect the damage to Bay Inn. For the most part it had come through well, but the crashing they'd heard in the wee hours was downed pine trees that had fallen all over the grounds. They were thankful the old live oaks and magnolias still stood.

"I think we're very fortunate not to have any more damage than this," Cole said.

"But I wish I'd had some of those pines taken down before now."

"Do you think the roads will be passable?" Thad asked.

Cole shrugged. "I don't know. Could be some lines down and trees lying across the road. There might be some flooding on our east side. I don't imagine any of that is going to keep you from making sure Dani is all right, though."

"You're right about that. I have to check on her, Cole."

"Well, hold on for a minute. I'll let Ronni know we're going."

"You don't have to come with me."

Cole started toward the house. "Oh, yeah, I do. We'll take my four-wheel drive." He pitched a set of keys to Thad. "Go ahead and start it up. I'll be right there."

By the time Thad started the vehicle and pulled it around to the back, Cole was waiting for him. Cole motioned for him to stay in the driver's seat and climbed in on the other side. "Let's go."

It took them twice as long as usual to get to town, with dodging fallen trees and electrical lines. There weren't many of those, though. By the time they reached the center of town the damage was more visible, and Thad prayed as they neared city hall.

The relief he felt when he saw it still standing was almost overwhelming. He swallowed around the huge lump in his throat as he put Cole's vehicle in park and jumped out.

He didn't know if Cole was with him or not. All he knew was that he had to find Dani as soon as possible. He went straight to her office but found it empty. He hurried to the bunker she'd shown him. She wasn't there, but one of the emergency team, who had been there when he'd brought the food the night before, asked, "May I help you, sir?"

"Can you tell me where I might find Miss Phillips?"

"I believe she's out with Chief Baker."

"Do you know where they went?"

"No. Probably downtown. I heard her talking about checking out things."

"Thanks." Thad headed back out into what had turned into a sunny day.

"Thad, wait up!" Cole called from behind him, and for the first time Thad realized Cole had been following him around city hall.

"I have to find her, Cole."

"I know you do. But she's all right, Thad. She's out checking on the damage. She wouldn't be doing that if she weren't."

Thad took a deep breath. Cole was right. She was okay. *Thank You, Lord.*

He nodded. "Thank you for making me realize that. I'm sure she has a lot to do. Maybe we'll run into her. In the meantime I guess we should see what we can do to help out."

"Okay." They took off walking down Bay Drive.

"Man, look at Beach Burgers," Cole said.

When he saw the damage to the small building, memories of having lunch there with Dani tugged at Thad's heart. "I hope it can be repaired."

They passed several businesses with shingles missing and trees leaning against them. Thad knew it could have been worse—and no doubt was worse down the coast. But he wouldn't breathe easy until he saw Dani and knew she was all right.

When he and Cole reached Meagan's Color Cottage, they were surprised to see Meagan and Nick already there.

"I thought you went up to Hide-a-Way Lake," Cole said.

"We did," Meagan said. "But once we knew the storm had passed we came back to check out the situation. Gram and Tori are still up there."

"Looks as if you fared pretty well," Cole said.

"The roof is damaged, but it doesn't appear to be too bad," Nick said. "The house is fine, and my office has a tree leaning on it. No real damage, though. We're definitely counting our blessings. How did the inn make out?"

"Pine trees down all over the grounds, but the inn came through pretty well. Same as you—we're missing some shingles, but I'm not complaining at this point. I was expecting much worse. Want some help taking off these boards?"

"That would be great. Thanks, guys."

"We stopped by city hall to see Dani earlier," Meagan said. "She was about to go out and take a look around, but she said we're really blessed. They've been getting reports from along the coast. Some of the restaurants and hotels were hurt pretty badly, and several casinos sustained a lot of damage."

Thad felt measurably better knowing Meagan had talked to Dani. It was all he could do to stay and help take plywood off the shop when he only wanted to comb the streets looking for Dani. He knew she was busy, and he'd promised not to get in her way, but—suddenly he thought how he could do something for her even if he couldn't see her yet. "When we get through here why don't we take the boards off Dani's place? I'm sure she'd appreciate it."

"I'm sure she would," Cole agreed. "Let's do that."

They made quick work of uncovering the windows to Meagan's shop, and while she checked on the inside Nick went with them to Dani's. Thad was relieved when he saw her place. Some shingles were missing, and two trees in her side yard were leaning against her roof—but if they were removed soon no real damage would be done. Her beautiful backyard was in fairly good shape, and he knew she'd be pleased.

After they took the boards off her windows and put away the plywood, they headed back to town. He was sad to see that while the Waters Flower Shop had survived with minimal damage, some of their hothouses out back had not.

Brad shrugged. "Plants can be replaced. We're all right; our home is fine. We're very thankful."

Thad was impressed with everyone's attitude and their willingness to pitch in and help others. As they headed back to city hall where Cole's vehicle was parked, Thad's heart beat faster with each step he took. Surely Dani would be back by now.

But she wasn't. The woman in charge at the front desk told them she'd gone to check on some of the outlying areas. "She mentioned wanting to see how Bay Inn fared."

Thad exchanged glances with Cole, and they dashed out of the building. Cole drove this time, and Thad prayed the whole way back to the inn. *Dear Lord, please let Dani still be there. Please let me hold her in my arms and know she's all right.*

A patrol car was parked outside the inn, and Thad's heart almost stopped when he saw Dani standing with the chief of police talking to Claudia and Ronni. Cole had barely put the brakes on before Thad was out of the vehicle.

Dani glanced their way, and for a moment time seemed to stand still for him.

"Thad!"

When she called his name, Thad hurried toward her. Dani ran to him, and when they met he scooped her up in his arms and whirled her around before finally letting her feet touch the ground.

"You're all right," they said in unison. Dani was crying and laughing all at the same time, and Thad didn't care who was watching. He leaned down and kissed her.

❧

Her heart feeling as if it were about to burst with happiness, Dani kissed Thad back. It was only when they realized they had an audience, by the applause from Cole and the chief, that they pulled apart.

"It's about time you two figured things out," Cole said. "I think we'll leave you alone for a while. I believe you have some things to discuss."

"Dani, I trust you have a way back to town, so I'm taking off," Chief Baker said, smiling. "It's about time to call it a day anyway."

"I probably need to get back to town." But her gaze never left Thad's.

"Dani," the chief said as he started toward the car. "The phone service isn't up yet, and the electricity is still out. You have some time here. Take advantage of it. But remember you've called for a dawn-to-dusk curfew for as long as the power is off. If you can't get back into town by dusk—"

"She'll stay here," Claudia said. "Don't worry about her, Harvey. We'll take good care of her."

"Thanks, Chief," Dani managed.

"You're welcome. You deserve a break. You did a great job, Dani." He looked at her and Thad and waved before turning his car around and heading back to town.

Dani felt awkward for a moment as Cole cleared his throat. "Aunt Claudia is determined not to lose any more food than necessary so we're going to light the grill. I think you two have some talking to do, so. . .we'll leave you to it and see you for dinner in a while."

"Thank you," Thad said, waving his friend away.

Dani chuckled. Ordinarily she'd have been embarrassed by having so many people witness her and Thad's reunion, but she was so happy and relieved to see him, so determined to let him know how she felt, that it didn't faze her. Besides, she knew they truly cared about the two of them. Still she didn't mind that they'd given them some privacy.

"I don't know how bad the path is, but we can see if we can get to the bay from here," Thad said, leading her to the walking path at the back of the inn. He gripped her hand tightly as they made their way around several downed trees. Oddly enough, the bench that normally sat overlooking the bay was still there. It had been thrown about, but it was intact.

Thad set it upright and back where it belonged then pulled Dani beside him. They gazed out over the bay. It was nearly back to normal now, signaling the storm was over and reminding Dani how thankful she was that her town had survived—especially that the man she loved was all right.

"Dani, I—"

Dani placed her fingertips on Thad's lips and looked at

him intently. "No. Let me go first, please, Thad."

He nodded, and she slid her fingers away from his lips and onto his cheek.

"I let you leave last night without telling you how I feel, and I don't want one more moment to pass without your knowing." She looked into his eyes, wanting him to know without a doubt that what she said next came from her heart. She took a deep breath. "I love you, too, Thad Cameron. With everything I am."

She could see the joy shining from his eyes as he took her hand and kissed it. "And I love you, Dani Phillips— more and more each and every day. Last night was the longest night in my life, and I hope never to spend another one like it."

"I feel the same way." She smiled at him. "I hope you keep your word and ask me to marry you as you said you would."

Thad was down on one knee before all her words were out. He took her hand in his and placed it on his heart. "I am a man of my word, Dani Phillips. I promise to love you for the rest of my life. And I'd like to do that right here in Magnolia Bay. We can live at your house or buy a new one. Or have Cole build us one. I don't care. Whatever you want—only, please, will you marry me?"

Much as she loved Magnolia Bay, Dani had been prepared to move to Dallas if she had to. But this man, this precious man, was giving her *her* heart's desire. . .a life with him in her hometown. "Oh, yes, Thad Cameron. I will marry you."

Thad stood and pulled her to her feet and into his arms. Dani thought her heart might melt with the love she felt as his lips claimed hers in a kiss that told her he meant every word.

He raised his head and looked into her eyes. "Have I ever told you I've spent a lot of time trying to put a name to the color of your eyes?"

"No, you never did." Dani felt breathless as he lowered his head once more. "Did you figure it out?"

His answer waited for one more kiss, and then he said, "No. But I'll be happy to spend the rest of my life trying."

As they turned and started back to the inn, she thanked the Lord for getting them through the storm and for letting her have a chance to tell this man how much she loved him. She'd be glad to spend the rest of *her* days making sure he never doubted it.

epilogue

April

Thad thought this day would never get here. So much had happened since he'd proposed to Dani. They'd been blessed that no other storms had come their way, for there was much cleanup to be done all along the coast from Hurricane Nell.

The damage to the east had been far more extensive than that in Magnolia Bay. He and Dani both cried the day they finally got a good look at the destruction Nell had brought with her. Recovery wouldn't be quick or easy, but they knew the people along the coast were up to the task.

Thad had never doubted for a moment his decision to make his home in Magnolia Bay as he watched the town he and Dani loved reach out to those less fortunate along the coast. Some people had opened their homes to those who'd lost theirs. Others had helped with cleanup and restoration where needed. Churches were assisting in all kinds of ways.

Watching the people of this town open their hearts and arms to those who needed a helping hand had finally given Thad a hook for his Magnolia Bay advertising campaign.

It truly was "The Town with Open Arms." And it was paying off.

Hearing how the town reached out to others had convinced several companies to relocate to Magnolia Bay, and the city council had no doubt more would come. Magnolia Bay would once again be a thriving small city.

The housing market was tightening up, as he'd known it would. But he and Dani had decided to keep her home. They had no reason not to—they both loved it.

Thad had rented office space not far from city hall, and he and Dani were looking forward to having lunch at Beach Burgers when it reopened in the summer.

They both had wanted to get married as soon as the threat of hurricane season was over, but with so much damage down the coast neither he nor Dani felt right taking off for a wedding trip when so much needed to be done. They decided on a spring wedding, hoping the coast recovery would be well underway by then.

Miss Claudia and the Bannisters had just about adopted him, insisting he stay with them until he and Dani were married. They refused to take money from him, but he finally convinced them to let him work up an advertising campaign for Bay Inn in exchange for his room and board.

Busy as life had been, it was hard to believe the day he'd been waiting months for was here. Dani had wanted them to say their vows in the very place where he'd proposed to her, with Ronni and Meagan as her attendants and Cole and Nick as his.

Now Dani walked toward him down the azalea-lined path

at Bay Inn, looking so beautiful she took his breath away. He couldn't stop looking at her as she slowly made her way to him. They turned toward the minister, and as they said their vows in front of him and what seemed like the whole town of Magnolia Bay, Thad knew she'd picked the perfect setting.

The minister pronounced them man and wife, and as Thad kissed Dani for the first time as his wife, he thanked the Lord for bringing him to this town and especially to this woman who fit so naturally into his open arms.

A Letter To Our Readers

Dear Reader:

In order that we might better contribute to your reading enjoyment, we would appreciate your taking a few minutes to respond to the following questions. We welcome your comments and read each form and letter we receive. When completed, please return to the following:

Fiction Editor
Heartsong Presents
PO Box 719
Uhrichsville, Ohio 44683

1. Did you enjoy reading *With Open Arms* by Janet Lee Barton?
   ❑ Very much! I would like to see more books by this author!
   ❑ Moderately. I would have enjoyed it more if

   _____

   _____

   _____

2. Are you a member of **Heartsong Presents**? ❑ Yes ❑ No
   If no, where did you purchase this book? _____

   _____

3. How would you rate, on a scale from 1 (poor) to 5 (superior), the cover design? _____

4. On a scale from 1 (poor) to 10 (superior), please rate the following elements.

   ____ Heroine   ____ Plot
   ____ Hero   ____ Inspirational theme
   ____ Setting   ____ Secondary characters

5. These characters were special because? _____

_____

_____

6. How has this book inspired your life? _____

_____

_____

7. What settings would you like to see covered in future **Heartsong Presents** books? _____

_____

_____

8. What are some inspirational themes you would like to see treated in future books? _____

_____

_____

9. Would you be interested in reading other **Heartsong Presents** titles? ❑ Yes   ❑ No

10. Please check your age range:
   ❑ Under 18   ❑ 18-24
   ❑ 25-34   ❑ 35-45
   ❑ 46-55   ❑ Over 55

Name _____

Occupation _____

Address _____

City, State, Zip _____

NEW MEXICO

3 stories in 1

The stories of three women, struggling with the harsh realities life has thrown their way, play out under the historic mysterious skies of Roswell, New Mexico.

Titles by author Janet Lee Barton include: *A Promise Made*, *A Place Called Home*, and *Making Amends*.

Historical, paperback, 352 pages, 5³⁄₁₆" x 8"

_____

Heartsong

HEARTSONG PRESENTS TITLES AVAILABLE NOW:

___HP469 *Beacon of Truth*, P. Griffin
___HP470 *Carolina Pride*, T. Fowler
___HP473 *The Wedding's On*, G. Sattler
___HP474 *You Can't Buy Love*, K. Y'Barbo
___HP477 *Extreme Grace*, T. Davis
___HP478 *Plain and Fancy*, W. E. Brunstetter
___HP481 *Unexpected Delivery*, C. M. Hake
___HP482 *Hand Quilted with Love*, J. Livingston
___HP485 *Ring of Hope*, B. L. Etchison
___HP486 *The Hope Chest*, W. E. Brunstetter
___HP489 *Over Her Head*, G. G. Martin
___HP490 *A Class of Her Own*, J. Thompson
___HP493 *Her Home or Her Heart*, K. Elaine
___HP494 *Mended Wheels*, A. Bell & J. Sagal
___HP497 *Flames of Deceit*, R. Dow & A. Snaden
___HP498 *Charade*, P. Humphrey
___HP501 *The Thrill of the Hunt*, T. H. Murray
___HP502 *Whole in One*, A. Ford
___HP505 *Happily Ever After*, M. Panagiotopoulos
___HP506 *Cords of Love*, L. A. Coleman
___HP509 *His Christmas Angel*, G. Sattler
___HP510 *Past the Ps Please*, Y. Lehman
___HP513 *Licorice Kisses*, D. Mills
___HP514 *Roger's Return*, M. Davis
___HP517 *The Neighborly Thing to Do*, W. E. Brunstetter
___HP518 *For a Father's Love*, J. A. Grote
___HP521 *Be My Valentine*, J. Livingston
___HP522 *Angel's Roost*, J. Spaeth
___HP525 *Game of Pretend*, J. Odell
___HP526 *In Search of Love*, C. Lynxwiler
___HP529 *Major League Dad*, K. Y'Barbo
___HP530 *Joe's Diner*, G. Sattler
___HP533 *On a Clear Day*, Y. Lehman
___HP534 *Term of Love*, M. Pittman Crane
___HP537 *Close Enough to Perfect*, T. Fowler
___HP538 *A Storybook Finish*, L. Bliss
___HP541 *The Summer Girl*, A. Boeshaar
___HP542 *Clowning Around*, W. E. Brunstetter
___HP545 *Love Is Patient*, C. M. Hake

___HP546 *Love Is Kind*, J. Livingston
___HP549 *Patchwork and Politics*, C. Lynxwiler
___HP550 *Woodhaven Acres*, B. Etchison
___HP553 *Bay Island*, B. Loughner
___HP554 *A Donut a Day*, G. Sattler
___HP557 *If You Please*, T. Davis
___HP558 *A Fairy Tale Romance*, M. Panagiotopoulos
___HP561 *Ton's Vow*, K. Cornelius
___HP562 *Family Ties*, J. L. Barton
___HP565 *An Unbreakable Hope*, K. Billerbeck
___HP566 *The Baby Quilt*, J. Livingston
___HP569 *Ageless Love*, L. Bliss
___HP570 *Beguiling Masquerade*, C. G. Page
___HP573 *In a Land Far Far Away*, M. Panagiotopoulos
___HP574 *Lambert's Pride*, L. A. Coleman and R. Hauck
___HP577 *Anita's Fortune*, K. Cornelius
___HP578 *The Birthday Wish*, J. Livingston
___HP581 *Love Online*, K. Billerbeck
___HP582 *The Long Ride Home*, A. Boeshaar
___HP585 *Compassion's Charm*, D. Mills
___HP586 *A Single Rose*, P. Griffin
___HP589 *Changing Seasons*, C. Reece and J. Reece-Demarco
___HP590 *Secret Admirer*, G. Sattler
___HP593 *Angel Incognito*, J. Thompson
___HP594 *Out on a Limb*, G. Gaymer Martin
___HP597 *Let My Heart Go*, B. Huston
___HP598 *More Than Friends*, T. H. Murray
___HP601 *Timing is Everything*, T. V. Bateman
___HP602 *Dandelion Bride*, J. Livingston
___HP605 *Picture Imperfect*, N. J. Farrier
___HP606 *Mary's Choice*, Kay Cornelius
___HP609 *Through the Fire*, C. Lynxwiler
___HP610 *Going Home*, W. E. Brunstetter
___HP613 *Chorus of One*, J. Thompson
___HP614 *Forever in My Heart*, L. Ford
___HP617 *Run Fast, My Love*, P. Griffin
___HP618 *One Last Christmas*, J. Livingston

(If ordering from this page, please remember to include it with the order form.)

Presents

___HP621 *Forever Friends*, T. H. Murray
___HP622 *Time Will Tell*, L. Bliss
___HP625 *Love's Image*, D. Mayne
___HP626 *Down From the Cross*, J. Livingston
___HP629 *Look to the Heart*, T. Fowler
___HP630 *The Flat Marriage Fix*, K. Hayse
___HP633 *Longing for Home*, C. Lynxwiler
___HP634 *The Child Is Mine*, M. Colvin
___HP637 *Mother's Day*, J. Livingston
___HP638 *Real Treasure*, T. Davis
___HP641 *The Pastor's Assignment*, K. O'Brien
___HP642 *What's Cooking*, G. Sattler
___HP645 *The Hunt for Home*, G. Aiken
___HP646 *On Her Own*, W. E. Brunstetter
___HP649 *4th of July*, J. Livingston
___HP650 *Romanian Rhapsody*, D. Franklin
___HP653 *Lakeside*, M. Davis
___HP654 *Alaska Summer*, M. H. Flinkman
___HP657 *Love Worth Finding*, C. M. Hake
___HP658 *Love Worth Keeping*, J. Livingston
___HP661 *Lambert's Code*, R. Hauck
___HP662 *Dear to Me*, W. E. Brunstetter
___HP665 *Bah Humbug, Mrs Scrooge*, J. Livingston
___HP666 *Sweet Charity*, J. Thompson
___HP669 *The Island*, M. Davis
___HP670 *Miss Menace*, N. Lavo
___HP673 *Flash Flood*, D. Mills
___HP674 *Allison's Journey*, W. E. Brunstetter
___HP677 *Banking on Love*, J. Thompson
___HP678 *Lambert's Peace*, R. Hauck
___HP681 *The Wish*, L. Bliss
___HP682 *The Grand Hotel*, M. Davis
___HP685 *Thunder Bay*, B. Loughner
___HP686 *Always a Bridesmaid*, A. Boeshaar
___HP689 *Unforgettable*, J. L. Barton
___HP690 *Heritage*, M. Davis
___HP693 *Dear John*, K. V. Sawyer
___HP694 *Riches of the Heart*, T. Davis
___HP697 *Dear Granny*, P. Griffin
___HP698 *With a Mother's Heart*, J. Livingston
___HP701 *Cry of My Heart*, L. Ford
___HP702 *Never Say Never*, L. N. Dooley
___HP705 *Listening to Her Heart*, J. Livingston
___HP706 *The Dwelling Place*, K. Miller
___HP709 *That Wilder Boy*, K. V. Sawyer
___HP710 *To Love Again*, J. L. Barton
___HP713 *Secondhand Heart*, J. Livingston
___HP714 *Anna's Journey*, N. Toback
___HP717 *Merely Players*, K. Kovach
___HP718 *In His Will*, C. Hake
___HP721 *Through His Grace*, K. Hake
___HP722 *Christmas Mommy*, T. Fowler
___HP725 *By His Hand*, J. Johnson
___HP726 *Promising Angela*, K. V. Sawyer

Great Inspirational Romance at a Great Price!

Heartsong Presents books are inspirational romances in contemporary and historical settings, designed to give you an enjoyable, spirit-lifting reading experience. You can choose wonderfully written titles from some of today's best authors like Andrea Boeshaar, Wanda E. Brunstetter, Yvonne Lehman, Joyce Livingston, and many others.

When ordering quantities less than twelve, above titles are $2.97 each.
Not all titles may be available at time of order.